Remnants of Glory

Angela C. Costello

Sometimes it floods into her dreams. She wakes up with tears in her eyes after a dream so vivid she feels like she is there once again. At other times, she remembers all that happened when she walks along the same streets where she once walked twenty years ago. Shirley remembers the people who meant so much back then, the people who still mean so much to her now. But now, there exists the artist's pure focus on the remnants of the essence of the dreams that were once palpable in those youthful days. Presented are the everlasting legacies. A chronology to denote an era that reflects changes of substantive complexities. George Orwell even with his far-reaching visions couldn't possibly imagine.

One: Take A Breath and Be Brave

Words of Valor: *The environment becomes the song that had to be sung.*
A message becomes clear that compromise is rewarded.
Predictions are overwhelmingly overrated at length.

`"Herein lies, measure for measure, Shirley Raymond, a true treasure."`

"That's what I want it to say on my epitaph!" shouted Shirley across the oily, slick, rain-soaked alleyway. Everyone else was drumming to their own beats and as thus, they were completely oblivious to her state of being. There were: Sharon, a pixie-styled girl from Victoria, Teresa, the bright eyed petite girl from Winnipeg, and of course, Larry, the outdoor explorer from Thunder Bay. Shirley had called them all together to celebrate her last night out in Vancouver for as yet an undetermined amount of time.

Sharon and Shirley had spent the last five years establishing the truest of friendships, and because of Sharon's west coast roots, Shirley wanted to know her more, since many of the people she had met were transplants from On-terrible, that festering province to the east. They two were on the spring-board toward the establishment of their adult lives, and above all were in need of each other.

Teresa and Larry had met Sharon and Shirley through their work at the Waterford Centre Hotel. Shirley was in room service, Sharon was a concierge, Teresa worked at the front desk, while Larry worked as a bellman. Larry had come to the coast from Thunder Bay – that western Ontario desolate point of no return – with the intention only to stay long enough to get in a little skiing, but as it turned out, he never returned to Thunder Bay.

The night was Friday the 13th of November. It was a full-on party kind of night due to the fact that the rain had stopped for two days in a row. It seemed as if everyone in Vancouver had come out to celebrate the weather. Larry raised a pint in the air at the Irish Steamboat Pub to christen these last few cherished moments with someone he had been able to trust the minute they had met. "SSSHHHirley! may the road rise to meet you!!!....," was the toast of the night. This chorus was started off by Sharon, naturally.

Sharon's parents ran a famous bed and breakfast on Vancouver Island. She was like a cheerleader for all good causes fresh and full of fun ideas. Shirley found her companionship was like much needed fresh air. They were able to spill their guts to one another without fear, judgment, nor recourse. Shirley and Sharon were always up to some kind of exciting adventure. Larry couldn't help himself when he would say; "You two are the most fun people to be around. I can't believe the mischievous energy that you two emit."

It was true, since Shirley had met Sharon, she hadn't ever had so much fun in her life. They would go to the hottest club in town and dance the night away, then stay up and talk each other to sleep. Talk? - no, more like laugh each other to sleep. In fact, in a moment of realization, Shirley felt that she had never laughed so much in her life. It was as if the past grief of loneliness was washed away the moment she was in the presence of her dear friend Sharon.

Teresa, on the other hand, was very timid. Sometimes she would speak so softly that Larry would bellow out, "What the?, Giddy y'up now!" Teresa was good to have around to balance out all these bouncy kind of characters whose minds had finished the bigger picture intrinsic to their exchanges before the words could come out. Teresa was one who took her time with her assessments, and then she would express herself.

Larry, Sharon, and Shirley all had their stories about the

first time they met Teresa. Theirs' was a peculiar solidarity. Teresa's opener would always be, "Do you know anyone who sells weed?" To look at her you would just be completely shocked at that. Teresa's demeanor was very plain, almost to the point of being dull; however, all her friends agreed that her heart was made of gold. That girl would drop everything at a hat, to help her family and friends out. She was known to drive through the paranormal winds like the gales of November in Manitoba. Just as natural as anything she would stop at nothing to help support someone in peril.

Though Winnipeg stood as the metropolis of Manitoba, sometimes in early springtime even on the west coast Teresa could hear that desolate prairie wind whistling through the depths of her soul. Her upbringing had influenced her to the point that she held in high regard all things lovely. Teresa's one great passion was fashion. She touted all the latest colours and hot trends everywhere she went. Her hair styles would enter the room before she would.

In her adolescent days, Teresa had found expression against the dull environment in which she found herself. This was all before she had made her way to Vancouver. Vancouver was another story all together. The beauty of the ocean, the mountains, and the trees were colossal; fresh produce was in abundance, everything was green all year round. She suddenly felt that different things had taken priority. The big hair wasn't really necessary against the backdrop of the dramatic oceanic views. The yearning for the expression of beauty was hardly necessary when beauty unfolded at every turn in this jewel of a city.

The Vancouver Public Library had just been built with much fanfare surrounding it. It took over the feel of the business core where the sprawling suburbs to the east funneled in towards the west, in an air of high drama. It appeared as an edifice of power, not as the slaughter house that it mimicked. Whoever the decision-makers may have been, one had to adore this choice for public space.

When she first stepped toward the front entrance it was if she were being swallowed up by this Roman Coliseum replica. It appeared so miraculously imposing. How strange that this remarkably gruesome remnant could be made into something so benign, fortifying, and educational. It would now symbolize a place where many people could learn, what better pass time could there be? "Have you been to the new library yet?" Shirley gleamed at all of her dear companions, but the question was particularly directed at Teresa. Teresa just gestured no because at her left shoulder was a very persistent yet alarmingly handsome man, staring into her eyes.

Teresa was just 5'2" but had the most distinctive sparkle in her eyes. Her mother had died when she was 4 years old, and now was the time for her to strike it out on her own, far away from all the turmoil of her life in Winnipeg. That sparkle in her eyes was a reflection of her genuine determination. "My dad used to tell me that I would never be able to leave the prairies, but I worked so hard at school that I earned a scholarship to Simon Fraser in the Engineering program," she told Larry once.

There weren't many girls at school for Teresa to become friends with given that her program was male dominated, so she had been relieved when she got her job at the Waterford. Shirley and Sharon were more than obliged to let her into their sisterhood circle. However, Teresa had kept her private life covert, only really opening up emotionally with Larry.

Larry was rough and ready for anything life passed his way almost to the point of being over the top. A stranger would wonder at the superlative pitch, and the brazen tone of his voice. It resonated as though Tarzan was hollering out through the jungle. Larry possessed a persistent immediate reaction to the truth of every situation, whether it were a past experience of painful proportions, or whether it seemed to be simply a matter of an expression of the present. This insight was good common sense. With unabashed vehemence, Larry would certainly offer his opinion of the predicaments that people had discovered, or that were yet to be acknowledged. It was an accepted truism that change was omnipresent in life. This was a fact that Larry unflinchingly supported if one ever found themselves among the people he cherished; one would consider his counsel a matter of course. Teresa felt safe in his presence although she often found herself the brunt of his disdain. However, like all people, Larry was flawed, and sometimes his uncensored wit would go against good judgment. After all, Larry was sure that his was the best point of view.

Teresa and Larry kind of spoke their own language, and when it came to hanging out Larry had felt protective toward Teresa. This instinct immediately kicked-in when he realized that she had moved out to Vancouver against her father's will. Teresa knew in her gut that Vancouver held the key to some higher career aspirations. Even if she were not to settle in Vancouver for the rest of her life, there was still something that had made her comfortable in for the most part, the downtown residential area of the Westend, but also in the west side neighbourhood of Kitsilano. That seemed to be the consensus of many of these young pioneers of the time. The girls had identified with the others who were recent transplants. They held a commonality in that they had reached a point in their lives when long-term commitments were yet to be written in stone.

Shirley had met Teresa after her three months probationary working period at the Waterford. She was busy making her schedule fit around her very busy social life. Vancouver's

Westend area was known for its unexpected surprises, especially west of Denman Street. Shirley had managed to rent a very comfortable flat right on the famous landmark Stanley Park, for heavens sake. Stanley Park was the centre of the universe down there. The seawall wound around the park in all it's majestic nature. It was the constant iron- clad reminder of the existence of the First Nations people of the Salish tribe who used to live upon her shores.

Whenever Shirley had felt alone, she would stand along the Stanley Park stretch of seawall adjacent to Third Beach, or she would strap on her roller blades, and stop to gaze at Siwash Rock. Third Beach jutted out as a bit of a small inlet between Stanley Park and the west side shores of Granville Island, Kitsilano, and the natural shores of Wreck Beach at U.B.C. Siwash Rock adorned the pinnacle of the seawall at Third Beach, and stood out as a spectacular anomaly. Its claim to fame was as the geologists suggest, that it was a fragment of an older sediment of stone.

Whatever its story, Siwash Rock was one lonely chunk of boulder with a deep humiliating narrative of its own. Thus it was the most distinctive rock in the Vancouver area – some kind of magical rock made of a more time-resistant form of volcanic stone; the only one of its kind, it bore itself well. The pride of its original inhabitants tells its story: *"Indian Legend Tells Us That This 50 Foot High Pinnacle of Rock Stands As An Imperishable Monument*

To Skalish The Unselfish Who Was Turned Into Stone By Q'As The Transformer As A Reward For His Unselfishness." The seawall became the ultimate leveler for Shirley in all its contrast to the glass and concrete bustle of the city. Stanley Park remains as it was – only now and then being churned by nature.

People have left their indelible impressions on the seawall, in every crevice, bend and surface, in every type of weather. Everyone would feel the ghost remnants of so many who had passed in all their fears, hopes, and dreams, and quietly one's soul would bear their eloquent narratives. Next to the ocean all could meditate amongst its' mystical landscapes, and wash away all that had gripped them. This was a stretch of solace, and of all the graces that the water would absorb. It was a place that was timeless, yet moved on with the times in harmony. It was not a place to wallow, nor feel sad about things that may have been.

As she skipped, walked, jogged, roller bladed or just sauntered around that spectacular lush carpet of wonders, her loneliness would wash away. Indeed, this was a piece of sanity where heaven, and earth met. In the sopping rain, and as every season unfolded, Shirley was drawn to the sanctity of the supernatural Stanley Park seawall. It was a place where she could perform a formal, thorough cleanse. It had occurred to her that with every curve she was awed by the stories of nature alongside those of human dignity.

The benches bore safe contemplative places where one could read about the dedications of a lifetime. Out there on the seawall, with ethereal beings, there was no time to wallow, no time to hide under the blankets, or to contemplate sorrow. There existed too many reminders out there to manifest what happiness there could be here, and now.

In the short five years that Shirley had been working at the Waterford, she was able to meet some fascinating friends, but not only that there were some triumphant visitors that showed up. Quite unexpectedly, Shirley delivered some tea, and toast to none other than Bob Hope. He was small, and quiet as a mouse when she came to the door. Those eyes that had witnessed so much had nothing to say. The face was unmistakable; shock set in with the thought that maybe she was seeing things at first. Another time, Pierre Trudeau walked through the lobby wearing a tweed cape. His walk was what had given him away, and really who else could pull off wearing a cape? Shirley scrambled the day that Wayne Gretzky stayed in the Royal Suite. He had ordered everything on the menu for breakfast. When she rolled the room service cart into his room, he answered the door. He wore nothing but a t-shirt and boxers. Her eyes glazed over when she handed him the bill. Much to her awkward embarrassment, with quiet indignation her hockey hero had recognized that dazed, and starry eyed look.

Now, after five years of serving the privileged and the

famous, this young woman trying to get her barrings had started to evaluate how she felt about her job there. There had been all the hard lifting, and running around. Somehow, even in her ruffled confusion, she knew that however difficult it would be, the time was right to shift gears. With attaining a comfortable position at one of the most prestigious hotels in Vancouver as her first accomplishment, it would not be an easy change, nor one that she would not second guess her self about later on. The emergent adult longed for a career where she would hold authority, one where she would be looked up to for using her intellect. This was a time of introspective journeys, a pivotal about-face moment ripe to occur. In fact, this was a point in the life journey when wrestling with fears became a full time activity. Within her own judicious framework she was eternally bound by nothing other than her primal instincts, which were in constant contradiction to her intellect. Chaos is all that she knew. Chaos was a form of reference, and in an odd sense, refuge.

Such is the complexity inherent in relationships, especially amongst a group of women. Teresa, for her part, was comforted having Shirley as her friend, but some of her own worst fears held her back from becoming too close to her. As chirpy as can be the duo of Shirley and Sharon were having one of their phone sessions when Shirley had said out of the blue, "Do you think Teresa maybe only comes across as being bland, or do you think that maybe she just is bland?" To which Sharon replied, "Well I did honestly notice that something about her is off, but don't tell anybody, this is between you and me, O.K?" Much as the act of gossiping is admonished to those of us with moral convictions, it happens with fervent frequency.

It wasn't that either Shirley or Sharon had meant to be cruel, it truly was just that people are naturally cruel toward each other sometimes. It would be hypocritical to think that there had never been times when they, as humans, had never been overly critical toward others. The question really was, would they be overt about this, or would they be purposely devious, and just smile in people's faces while thinking about these things.

Values are expendable if they are just written down on paper, or if contemplated in theory. It's true, Shirley and Sharon could have stood to have more compassion toward Teresa. However, this condemnation that Teresa was setting herself up to endure was about to be fatefully resolved. Shirley had decided that after five years of working at one of the most prestigious hotels in the city, that it was time to travel the world, to see some other places. Feeling this way made it a lucky time for her that she had some relatives to go and live with in Buenos Aires, Argentina.

From Vancouver to Buenos Aires

When the topic of Buenos Aires had first been brought up, Shirley knew that she hadn't even heard of the city except through the first Broadway release of ***Evita***, the musical. Evita was an historical figure of epic proportions. Her life was full of intrigue, romance, violence, combat, and ultimately her very public battle with cancer. The musical had made an indelible impression on a generation in conflict with itself through the Cold War Era.

So, with very little realistic agenda in mind, off the young lady went full, stock, and barrel into a shiny night. Although Shirley and Sharon would remain the best of friends, realistically circumstances do tend to change people, as well as their sense of direction. What Shirley was not comprehensive of was that living far away in another country is for the most part an internal, profoundly painful process.

Argentina was on another continent altogether. There would be no glaring familiarity in South America. For one thing, the reality of the situation was that she would be desperately isolated, and a great distance away. One would guess that she would have the logical faculties to absorb the gravity of this move. However, life had gone stale for her of late, the intensity of this process was something that was longed for at this point in her life.

With Shirley gone from Vancouver, Sharon and Teresa

would become invaluable to each other. Theirs had the potential to become a fellowship of warmth, and Larry was mentally prepared to help fill the gap as well. These were people driven together by chosen circumstances. All of them were in their twenties, had moved away from their immediate families, and were deciding really who they wanted to be. It was a time in their lives when they could shed the futile experiences of the past, and move toward being their most authentic selves.

Friends came and went in these types of circles; however, the bonds were undeniable. Theirs' were the types of bonds that could overcome the boundaries of geography. Moving to a completely different landscape with separate past histories made these friends feel their regional diversities at times. Shirley had traveled from a very young age, having had family who were able to provide her with a place to stay, and a really good reason to go.

Sharon, on the other hand, had been quite protective of her west coast heritage. The Canadian west coast wasn't a place that one moved away from. In Sharon's case, the natural environment was precious, what no one could take away from her life. The protectionist west coast sentiments were simmering. Therefore, B.C. was not an easy place to feel at home in after Expo86. The winds of progress were in a real sense, opening a channel to the Eastern world, and that was not always easy for the native Vancouverites to adjust to. Not only was Vancouver being flooded by immigration, but at the same time, these young lost souls were moving in from all over Canada. This pocket of land was actively being bombarded by people from all over the place.

The true Vancouverites living in the Westend were few, and far between in 1991. There were locals there; some hidden away in their quiet suburbs, some aghast at the way that their perfect sized city, in the mildest climate in all of Canada, was becoming the destination of young Easterners who fell in love when they first glimpsed its shores. These Easterners came from all types of backgrounds; some were straight out of university, such as the gang that found themselves working at the Waterford. At this time, the provincial protectionism that was slowly eroding for Vancouverites was not in its infancy in the early 90's.

All at the same point in time, the political fortitude, and the distance between the provinces were but a backdrop to the influx of affluent Asian immigrants. Therefore, in the last decade of the twentieth century, people from the other Canadian provinces would have to be of the hardiest stock if they were to truly call Vancouver B.C. home. The eyes of the wealthy landowners who had carved out their stake in the province from birth could bore a hole right into them. The wealthy settlers were diligent about protecting their economy in British Columbia, wanting to attract more people who could make a substantial contribution to it. Yet alongside this sentiment was an ever strong, constantly burning hippie environmental revolution.

Vancouver is substantially a modern bustling, cultural mosaic to be clear, one with big visionary plans. The citizens making the decisions could see all points of view very clearly, in openly public consistent dialogues. Maverick scientist David Suzuki forged on with his heavily perceptible influences. In 1991, with Nirvana as their back ground music, there never really was a plan for ten, or twenty years into the future for these young working class Canadians who were embarking on the beginning of their lives. These 20 somethings of the 1990s opted to burst out into the world, as quickly as possible, with a spirit of abandon.

Vancouver downtown was set up for the transient mobile people due to the fact that owning property was way beyond what normal people could afford – and still is. It was tiresome when at this young age an individual did not feel safe, and comforted by barely making a daily existence. With all its toil at this given point, a sense of being was not tied to the long haul of future decades. It was as though this was the moment to be seized, with all of the energy one could hope never to let go.

It was difficult not to enjoy the strength that a long tranquil sleep could bring, with the restlessness of the moment always upon the mind. Vancouver as a setting, opened the untrained eye to an ever widening perspective. There were the ongoing promises of tasting foods, of new exotic spices, and of having a drink of sustenance that one had never had the pleasure of before. Around every corner of moving to the city of Vancouver at such a rapturous age, were fortifying, though edifying pleasures.

Once the dawn arose during this time one would blaze on to the next adventure. At night all was intensified. There hardly seemed to be a break upon the horizon, yet pain was always near. So as thus, Shirley and her Vancouver family held on sweetly. They were dancing in the dark metaphorically speaking. They would hold their breath to see what was around the next corner.

There was so much to discover there in Vancouver that one knew that years would go by before one could uncover everything. Intimacies with new circumstances transform people. Shirley was slowly transcending all of the novice exposures into her artistic sensibilities. They were embodied side by side to her depths.

Looking like he were traveling in a modern day chuck wagon, Larry had driven out to Vancouver in his 1974 red Ford pickup with the topper on the back. Clearly everyone could see him coming. What a sight that was! After living in Thunder Bay all his life up to then, he swiftly decided during the beginning of ski season that he would drive out to the coast to go skiing for a couple of weeks. It didn't quite happen that way, but when a man is only 22 years old, there usually aren't outside forces in his life that would tie him down. When Larry, who had been known to spend every moment he could camping in the great outdoors, drove through the Rockies to the west coast, it was beyond words what was going through his mind in a millennium leap-ahead mode.

The mountains felt like they were protecting him with the dazzling display of their splendour, such that defied apt descriptions. Larry wrote down all the names of the towns that he had driven through to keep as a reminder of this sprawling natural wonder that every human being is able to freely appreciate. He drove through Hope, B.C. astonished by the missing mountain, and contemplated about how harsh Mother Nature could be to suddenly gouge out such a huge crater of rock in one split second. How loud the sound of the mudslide must have been if it were recorded; he wondered how far it would have resounded.

The province of British Columbia presents as a precious jewel on the crown of the entire country of Canada. No one visiting for the first time could deny it. Ontario has its' bush' - its own brand of tundra – and magnificently exposed bits of the Canadian Shield. These are the characteristic elements of wonder that present as remnants in its story of what was once so long ago.

Thunder Bay, Ontario had shown its particularly harsh climate for Larry just before he left. The tundra-like qualities of the area in winter had beautiful aspects on display right alongside its most harsh aspects. However, Larry never forgave the way the air there felt upon his skin in that endless winter; with the hair lining his nose freezing when he walked outside. In the midst of desolation, the pulp mill oozed its stench all through the village that was so blatantly split in two. The young adventurer knew instinctively that it would be worth it for him to begin to see more places outside the town of Thunder Bay.

Thunder Bay Ontario is right in the middle of nowhere, with Winnipeg being the closest city, and still yet a lengthy six hour drive. What Larry was not completely prepared for was how uplifting it would be for his spirit to live in Vancouver. There was a connection between him, the ocean, and the mountains. He was like an older brother to his Waterford Hotel friends, even though he was only two years their senior. This young man would have wanted to date them all, if he didn't work with them every day. Larry adored all of them in their own way, and without family close by, it was nice to have a pack to be the brother wolf with. After all, who else would be bystanders to his inner lion's roar?

Things became complicated when he dated Cathy, one of the bus-girls. After three months of hot, and heavy dating between the two of them, Cathy fooled around with the head chef. It was a disgraceful thing because Larry caught them at the Waterford Christmas party. She was getting busy in the men's washroom, and Larry just happened to walk in. After that bleep on the radar, Larry thought it was better that he just be good friends with Shirley, Sharon, and Teresa. He made the connection that indiscretions led to scandals. He didn't need to be girl crazy.

Vancouver was like an amusement park for an avid outdoors man. There was an endless array of activities right there all around. Larry would run up and down the Grouse Grind, kayak in Deep Cove, surf in Tofino, ski in Whistler, snow shoe at Mount Seymour, go fishing at Chilliwack River, and participate in just about every camping trip that he could muster.

The most memorable trip arranged by Larry and his Vancouver friends was the camping trip at the glacial lake on Mount Garibaldi the summer before. This was an easy steady incline trail of three and half hours. All six campers had packed lightly all except for Shirley and Sharon, of course, who brought the party favours consisting of: red wine, and beer.

Larry was the camping organizer for many of the people who worked at the hotel. Another event he organized was a skydiving excursion to Chilliwack with 15 other people who worked at the Waterford. It was a resounding success, even though most in the group were hung over from the party at the sous chef's house the night before. Shirley was a good sport for most of the day. Even after six hours of training, and practice drills – once that airplane door opened she just decided from her gut that she couldn't do it. "It's too scary." She chimed above the roar of the plane's engine.

This was a prime example, there was something so irrational to her line of thinking that annoyed Larry, but at the same time it was one of her traits that he was most attracted to. The secret to this girl was that she didn't want to assert herself too much because she really just wanted people to like her. This was part of her ruin. To really make sure to stay centred, it isn't the best policy to be vulnerable to the whims of others. This balance is something that Shirley had struggled with most of her life, and it would continue to disrupt things for her. Like many people in this predicament, they never took the time to actually focus on what they truly wanted. It had been her lot in life to be surrounded by unsolicited advice day in, and day out, all through her early years. With all those voices in her head nagging at her about not doing this, and really aimed along the lines of what not to do, it's not wonder that she really didn't know what to do.

Making important decisions were not like second nature to her. What was indeed natural, however, was to keep moving, going in a forward motion. The entire idea of hope meant that the future had to look better than the present, and the past. Unwittingly, her keen insightful senses skewed her perceptions of reality. In some ways it could produce positive outcomes but often it did not. Hope, therefore, became a manifestation of constant disappointment to this young woman. The thought processes involved in the concept of hope are intrinsically vicarious. One comes to the end of their metaphorical rope before they can embrace hope.

Teresa interrupted the sound of the smash of the glasses behind them by hollering out to Shirley, "I hope you packed lightly." "For sure!" said Shirley. This remarkable woman had been a warrior princess when it came to being prepared on any sort of tour she had made in her short, but well-traveled existence.

She came across as a high maintenance impractical type. In all her years were there only but a few people who didn't notice something about her? Shirley wasn't the girl who floated off from your consciousness. There was something about the expressive nature that she had, which people immediately took notice of. "I am very sensitive." This was a phrase that she would hear herself say in her most complex hours. The reaction she would get for the most part was utter denial. She was the woman whom people admired for her internal strength. That strength was a survival tactic that came out through her unending curiosities. It was a different sort of intelligence that she possessed one based on survival; such a basic instinct. It came out in her voice; her manner of speaking would be full of emotional conviction even in the most laid back circumstances. Many people are understood for their sensitive nature. Shirley was misunderstood for the most part. She felt that this was what had made her the most vulnerable. Being alone was miserable for her, but she couldn't find a productive way to be in a tight wound relationship as yet. Maybe it would happen, and perhaps not.

The thought of Buenos Aires in the midst of her inner journey;

the home of "Evita" was an attractive thought. Shirley's practical nature knew that it would be a far away place with a different language, and culture, but what really took over for her were the romantic images of tango dancers, sexy cafes, and a modern, flashy metropolis.

This night along the shores of the Georgia Straight, was over when the conversations went from fluffy airy things like make-up, to what time everyone had to get up the next morning. Reality has a way of ruining the present drifting moods. Sharon and Shirley bolstered each other flagrantly in the enjoyment of the moment. It was as if they were setting the stage so that everyone else in their presence would drift right into this safe world of their own making.

Sharon was just about sick inside when she tried to think about not being around Shirley. It had felt like a fateful friendship from the start. Both had felt removed from people at the time, and together with this in common they brought each other back into the human fold cackling like a couple of chickens. The shared laughter had a deep resounding effect on Shirley. In first point of contact some observers were taken aback by the emotive force of their laughter. Sharon was just loud like that, but she had certainly earned herself a chorus when she met her dear friend Shirley. The pair were so interesting to watch. It was like a traveling unpredictably fascinating circus act. Fresh as daisies the next morning, Sharon had borrowed her new boyfriend's car to take her dear close friend to the airport.

Two: So What's New? Everything.

Words of Valor: Putting oneself out of context is, in fact, a dramatic experience.
To gain proper perspective, the past is worth transcending.
Hearts full of wishes are bound to be broken.

Shirley had to fly from Vancouver, through to Toronto, Sao Paolo, and finally, Buenos Aires. It was a long haul. It was her primere flight to South America. The airplane was actually flying nose first in a decidedly downward direction. It was an enormously enjoyable flight because she felt a sense of safety within the company that she was in. There was an unspoken sense of her hovering above the earth on a cloud of serenity. There would be so many exciting things that she would partake in for the first time. It was beyond words what her mind processed during those moments before she stepped onto Argentine soil.

Her relatives made it possible for her to sit in Business Class; a treatment that she had never had before. It was as though the flight attendants could read people's vibes, and they unobtrusively would react to every slight move. Mind boggling, all this action, and reaction without words. However there was still a sense of ease all around. In deeper context, travel makes one aware of their cultural acuity.

Like all first time experiences, there is a certain pause that takes place at first contact with a new culture that ensures that the observer is part of the pulse of the action, without having to participate. In the name of true fellowship the pilot of the aircraft carrying Shirley and her six relatives invited them all to experience the voyage through his senses. They were carefully ushered into the cockpit as they were flying through the Caribbean Islands, and with almost an agonizing longing, gazed up through the glass into the sparkling sky. The canvas overhead had enveloped them in all its natural glory.

So, with such a smooth voyage to start with, the next phase of the trip sent shock waves through her very skin. The descent into Sao Paolo, Brazil, was one view that was unprecedented in her life. There seemed to be an unending stream of gray concrete skyscrapers outside her window. In fact, to Shirley the concrete was everywhere, as far as her eyes could tell there was not a single patch of green area to be seen. The moment was frozen in time burning a hot ember into her mind. She hoped against all hope that Buenos Aires wouldn't be so imposing. There would be times far into the future that through awe she close her eyes, to see that image. Concrete skyscrapers on tiny patches of land with not one natural feature on the horizon. This memory retrieval capacity that all are born with was the one characteristic that served her the best.

The enlightened mind is acutely aware of more than just the images of one's surroundings; it also has the capacity to delve into what was beneath the surface; the essence of the real. This power when not used properly, is something that can make us restless. With the opening of horizons, the idea of the simple life wasn't one she could see as being worthy for her. It was a comforting thought to know that it existed as a point of reference, but she knew that it wasn't something that she could participate in. Buenos Aires represented this evolution of being separated, of standing out, and not fitting in with the status quo.

The plane landed at the airport finally, but immediately, she was arrested by the sounds and the multitude of drivers holding signs, yelling, and half paved highways, it was not the luxurious setting of her simplistic dreams. There we go getting carried away with phantom thoughts. The drive into Buenos Aires took over two hours at a velocity one didn't even know was possible on land, there they are being whisked away into the fray of chaos. It was like being thrown into a tub full of ice cubes.

It can be difficult for one to sit down with a map, or to not be so distracted as to ask for proper directions. This methodical way of making the most of time is not something that some of us are so sure about. Added to a feeling of being lost it was doubly frustrating at first because no one who took the public transit system spoke a word of English; some were dirt poor indicated by all the worldly possessions they had on their backs. Unlike in good old Canada, the class lines were drawn boldly in this country. Buenos Aires was over run by immigrants from Paraguay, and Bolivia living in their barrios sectioned off from the rest of the civilization that surrounded them. These were the people on the edges of civilization, who made a living any way that they could. The pay scale for them was the equivalent of two dollars a day, and on that they had to live in what was once the richest city on earth.

The juxtaposition of these two worlds was alarming to this young hopeful girl from privileged Canada. It jarred her alive in this world seething with uncertainty. Walking into the city all on her own she felt so lost, so lonely, and so afraid. The streets were narrow, dirty and noisy, all of them had long intimidating names of military generals, and they were tricky to navigate with changes in all directions, not to mention name changes along the way.

Buenos Aires with its highly spread out neighbourhoods, its French colonial crumbling charm was a city that once was, and now appeared to be, developing in its own sporadic manner. Although the immigrants had added to the cultural richness of the city, it was apparent that they were not acknowledged in a manner of togetherness. The dark skinned new comers were not there to fit in with the rest of the society. The hierarchy was stiffly in a place where it was not looking to be removed from for any perceived time in the future. In contrast to all that she had known, the reality of social placement was harsh, and severe. Since going out on her own was so jarring to her internal sensitivities, during the initial stages of her living there, Shirley considered that she was lucky to have family with whom she could stay. Her aunt Patsy and uncle Rob were placed there on an assignment to work with a multinational corporation to help with the marketing of pharmaceuticals. Patsy was very happy to have Shirley with them to help her out with her three children. The living quarters provided were spacious, and even decadent in ways. The house was equipped with eight bathrooms, a fireplace that a six foot man could stand in, a pool, and each room with its own balcony. No doubt that Shirley had to switch gears every where she turned right from the minute she landed. First of all, not only adjusting to the surrounding city but to living with a young busy family, with priorities not exactly in line with a 20 something on a quest to become her most authentic self.

The living arrangements became the trickiest of all adjustments. It was not that Shirley was a particularly selfish individual, this was not ever her intent, it was just that her entire life had been spent living as a fiercely independent person; one who didn't even have a mother to tell her what to do. Patsy, on the other hand, was the woman of the household which was her most precious domain, and that she was highly skilled at. Without the means to leave the country it was up to Shirley to make a go of Buenos Aires on her own terms. This was a hefty thing that she had to do. It was like jumping from a bridge with no landing gear. Change was painful at the best of times, and the further that people are driven out of their comfort zones the more difficult it can be.

The first day out on her own after only being surrounded by her house mates' familiar faces; Shirley was dropped out into the mean streets of the centre of Buenos Aires during midday. She was never one to have a keen sense of where she was, nor really did she previously need to have compass-like skills. In all her life she was able to get away with being on trips to Thailand, and throughout many countries in Europe, and of course all through Canada a few times, without actually having to drive, or take note of where to turn. Amazing how that was, now she had not a single idea where she was heading in this decaying, overbearingly loud, and chaotic city.

Buenos Aires on a hot day in the highest humidity was not a place a pedestrian who didn't have a clue where she was going wanted to be. She turned her head up to the street signs that looked entirely unique; each street was completely different from one another. Nothing looked familiar to her, the diesel fueled cars, and trucks were ancient. Some of the green Ford Falcons which were circa 1980s issue were still around, heavy as tanks, and still driving through the hollow pot holed streets. They were ominous reminders of the military strong hold that plagued Argentina for years. Notwithstanding, there were trucks driving around from the 1920s with wooden trim. This material sense of disconnectedness was emblematic of what it felt like to be Shirley in her deepest soul.

There was a need to belong, to fit in, but there was a strong pull for her not to be congruent; to somehow be disconnected. It was hard for her to stay focused, suddenly she turned into the entrance of the Britannia Business English School. She was greeted face to face by an elderly British man lost in the fray; who gave her an American history book that looked like it was designed for high schools in the United States in the 1950s, and was told that she had a job that afternoon. His desk, and his hair were disheveled, he looked like a relic from another time; there was such a state of shock going through her veins that her cognition couldn't muster a state of normalcy.

It was under such arresting terms that she would find herself unable to focus on what people were saying. With no training, without understanding a word of Spanish, not knowing where she was in this confusing city of sensory overload, she was going to teach two English classes one would be four hours after the other. This was a Canadian girl stifled by all of her comforting fears enveloping her, one was actually staring at her in the face. The lost girl did not know a soul, did not have a clue how to teach; her body was going to do something she was not even sure she wanted to do.

After many shallow breaths, her body moved into the narrow hollow streets. Despite a distinct tingling sensation in her limbs, making the most of the jam she was in, she made her way to the first English class. It was cause for concern when she arrived at the office of a man with five names, an older man at that, well into his 50s, who sat at a desk across from her, who was armed with nothing but an American history book with its cheesy fake illustrations. The smell of the office was vulgar from indoor cigarette smoking.

It was obvious when she stepped into a bank that Buenos Aires still maintained its stance on cigarette bylaws. After walking beside heavily armed guards, the tellers were behind thick acrylic shields with cigarette, and ashtray in strategic close proximity to their hands. This new experience was a moment frozen in time that would give one pause, for this was a clear indicator to make one aware; that this was such a brazen step made timidly. The hour was barely remembered except that it was one of the most uncomfortable ones in her life. The man across the desk, kept the same expression just like he was a zombie staring at her right in the eyes as she read from the book, and he remained silent. Not one word was actually exchanged between the two of them.

So when you go into a job interview and it lasts for about fifteen minutes and afterward you feel as though you are confused, but somehow by some strange turn of events, you have the job. This type of situation is one that you are not sure you want to be in, it is as though you have been fooled into taking the job. These are the types of jobs that this woman had thought she had surpassed in her life up until this moment. She had had several unremarkable survival jobs, and made the most of the cruel monotony. In some ways, the most talented of us are like slaves.

Buenos Aires was yet to be discovered, but this confused type of state that she found herself in, was just on the outset of her journey there. The tingling sensations lingered, however, in surprising ways throughout the two years in Buenos Aires. The year was 1996, the world was still innocent in many regions but the devastation of the Dirty War sizzled on in the Argentina's recent memories. The gangster war lord Menem who disguised himself as an economist, was still in power. There were news stories still being splashed on headlines revealing the latest Menem fueled violent scandal.

As Shirley's Castellano linguistic skills were finally kicking in, she realized that there were billboards at the train stations appealing to the public with the photos of missing journalists. This was to have been a thing of the past, but continued right up until the present day. Argentina had felt the pain of the Dirty War years since the 1980s, and was still living in the midst of fear. The Dirty War still existed after all. As she lived amongst the Argentines it wasn't until after that first year that Shirley started to truly understand their culture. How was it that in a place with so much pride, joy, and love could be host to so much corrupt infrastructure.

Taking a deep gaze into Argentine political history, gave light to this complexity. The Argentines considered themselves the uppermost congenial, and civilized of all the South American countries. That overweening pride was often a sore contention for

Shirley, as she politely tried to navigate her way through the city, and was not often treated kindly. Buenos Aires is a big city in comparison to Vancouver so this was one of the reasons why people were not so friendly. Who would even dare to compare such different contexts? Argentines in fact seemed sullen, or was it was just that they were demure? It was so difficult to tell which. They were probably a mixture of both. Antonio Banderas adorned a billboard advertising none other than cigarettes! He looked absolutely stunning too, one would have to think that could hardly be legal by Canadian standards.

It was indeed evident that the well educated Argentines who groomed themselves in the highest of styles, and with such conscientiousness, could feel doomed by their circumstances. In stark contrast sits the mindset of the extraordinarily ordinary Canadian culture. Shirley was often confronted by the fact that, Canadians are the darlings of the world in many respects.

In this context, she was completely out on a limb, especially when she had to live amongst both the common Argentines, and the wealthy ones. It was perfectly excusable to be disoriented when stepping into somewhere so away from anything experienced before. Like many young ladies, this one hadn't learned to forgive herself sometimes. The survival instinct was put above, and beyond what she had come to mature into, which were to give herself some slack. There was an inherent guilt that permeated every fiber of her being that made her feel insignificantly small.

However, this was a work in progress, the abilities that Shirley was not in possession of at this point in her life, were about to be honed.

At the end of that first day of work, having taken the hour and a half train ride back into the suburbs of the gated protected community of San Isidro Chico; she had to accept that Argentina was not going to be an easy place to adjust to. It was right from the first few moments in the home, and on the streets, that she was the outsider no matter where in that setting. To make the best of an inevitable situation knowing full well that she wouldn't be back in Canada for a long time to come; she endeavored to find full time work. This was no small undertaking, there were no regular people in Argentina who had come from little to rise above their stations in life.

The plight of the people had been played out on the world stage for all to see. Argentines were keen in knowing that the remnants of another time, and place had put them face to face with the gravity of the fact that the glory days were stained forever by the blood of their own humiliated people. The foreigners really had no right to be there in the eyes of the people. Their faces were full of sullen thoughts when they would recognize Shirley as a Canadian. If there was any comfort in not belonging, she had to be quite aware that she, of all people, would be able to find it.

"Como Estan" sounded more like "Come on Down", and in the Latin world of languages the Argentines were known to have peculiar accents, and they spoke at an extremely fast pace. By the tone of people's expressions the outsider's natural first thought would be that they were constantly mad at each other. One then became more familiar with expressions of the people, and thought they were being very warm, and friendly. Then in progression from that thought, one then understood just exactly what it was that they were saying, and in one instance with the removal of the language barrier, she realized that she was being publicly called a crazy lady. This came out of a woman on the train when Shirley dressed in her jogging gear to meet up with a bunch of foreigners who were in a running club. Apparently, the Argentines didn't like to see a young lady dressed in pajama like athletic gear. It just wasn't proper to appear in public like a slouch.

The inherent pain worn on the sleeves of the "Las Malvinas" war veteran was plainly demonstrated through his pitch; his speech, on the rapid train from the burbs into the city daily. He would shout at the top of his lungs while walking down the aisles about his hardships, and at the end of his emotional tirade would ask the riders for donations. He sounded as though he would burst into tears.

She heard the painfully honest cries of, "The Mothers of The Disappeared" rally in front of the "Casa Rosada" government house every Thursday. The group sold t-shirts, and walked around with signs recanting that they would never forget about the diabolical torture of their sons and daughters. This brimming city of 12 million had enough going on to make the head swoon. These were the streets worn down by history, one which could be felt around every corner.

Sometimes it felt as though one were on the set of a movie of the 1920s; with shops brimming with many gramophones. These old beautifully carved machines weren't even preserved under glass they still played music! The ghosts of the past lived in the present. Maybe some of the Nazi gold was being showcased in a shop window. The city certainly had a sad sorrowful soul. In San Telmo, the artists skillfully worked in their centuries old store fronts where one could always be caught off guard by the intricate beauty of their wares. Great attention was paid to details.

As thus, a foreign young single woman with no family, and no children really stood out as awkward among the crowds in Buenos Aires. This fact was so unexpected for Shirley being from good moral backing herself. It had never occurred to her that she could be looked down upon solely for being single. If an Argentine girl was in her 20s any one there would know that she just had to be married, or close to it. This woman represented the other end of the spectrum as she was not even in the running for marriage. The institution of marriage never was a priority.

Shirley was having enough of a difficult time finding a man who would stick by her. She was dumped every time she was even close to having a relationship with a man. She felt like a fool with men. She let them in on her vulnerabilities right from the moment she met someone new. Men had often made her feel inferior, needy, clingy, and very insecure about herself. There were hours when she would close herself off from the rest of the world, and stay with those thoughts, and visualizations of being in a ridiculously romantic relationship with a man of her fantasies. She had several flights of fancy, hockey players, the star of her favourite soap opera, the man at the bank, anyone that she would not have to live a reality with.

The one thread that remained true no matter what man was in her mind is that he was a true gentleman refined in manner and respect. There was nothing else that she wanted more than anything else in the man that she would fall in love with; is just that he would be of the highest of manners. There was something more refined about the Argentine men that truly attracted Shirley, and it was their manner of dress so debonair, and the way that they danced with light elegant ease. Buenos Aires was known the world over for its dance culture. The tango is in every expression of the city that it can possibly be.

The first days in Buenos Aires come alive when you become a spectator at one of the several tango venues. The dance itself is indescribable. Whether it's a formal type of club or informal, it really doesn't matter the mystique of the tango lives on in every crevice. This is something that was savoured with every sense of her soul that no matter what part of Buenos Aires she was in; one could feel the vibrations of the tango. Sultry, angry, chaotic, exhausting, refined, pleasurable, twisted, tapping, walking on the air that surrounds you; there is no getting away from the feeling of the tango.

For moments when Shirley lived in the city she would close her eyes to feel and see the sights of the tango, even if they weren't there for the naked eye she knew, that its' essence would stay with her long after she left Buenos Aires. It was a plaintive cry, please never let me let go of this feeling, she would plead. This was the element of Argentina that she felt a sense of comfort with the most. The large pampas with their wide empty spaces didn't appeal to her with its images of ranchers, their ropes, their horses and their sing songs by the open fire, were not in her fondest dreams. She dreamed instead of a night on the town wearing one of the many high fashion power suits with the skirt up above the knee, and the jacket hitting all the proper curves of her body. These would be complete along with the skyscraper high heels that all of the Argentine women were sporting.

Argentine women were a tough crowd to compete with for the single attractive Canadian female. Not only were the women of Buenos Aires touted as being the most beautiful women on the South American continent, but on every continent for that matter; they had plenty of attitude packed in their beauty kits as well.

Never had Shirley heard women speak with such strong punctuation, and emphasis. She was not cognizant at first of exactly what they were saying, that came later on, but at first she just thought every thing that they were talking about they must have on great authority, just by the tone of it. Either the Argentine women were very feisty, or they were just highly expressive, it was confusing for the outsider to observe them. They all looked like they just stepped out of a spa with their perfect long hair, long cat like claws, skinny bodies, and always high heels, sexy skanky high heels. The men of Argentina seemed to fade into the back ground under their fedoras; it was the women that really stood out. A lot of women were it seemed, perched for their turn on the runway in a competition to see who could look the most stunningly fashionable.

This Canadian girl could fit in with these women, but it was just their model like skinny bodies that made her look like she might not actually be an Argentine. It was peculiar that on one day during her first month of living there that she was stopped and asked directions. The irony was that she wouldn't even be able to tell people where to go even if she did speak Spanish. Somehow that one brief encounter was but one time in public that she felt that she may fit in.

There were so many heavily woven threads of frequencies to tune into. The Argentine language, well it wasn't typical Spanish as one would hear in Mexico, or in Spain. The Argentines spoke unreasonably fast, and used different expressions. They were special people that were not just of Spanish descent, but to a greater extent most of the early settlers were from Italy who steadily immigrated with a great influx after World War II when the old world mother country was reduced to rubble. This intricate Italian infusion, along with the fact that Argentina is located so far away from all other countries make the accent hard to decipher.

Her perceptions were not as honed as they would have to become. In fact, there was an element of newness to all of her perceptions at once. Immersion of that sort was difficult to describe, and certainly individualistic. Best to say, that her body took itself through the cultural dissonance in stages, for it was too much to bear all at once. Shirley was particularly sensitive to how she might present herself to the native Castelleno speakers using their high styled language. Greetings amongst Argentines were formally strict no matter what social, or public situation that a person would find themselves in.

For instance, if you didn't greet a stranger by first using the time of day many would not want to respond. A lot of the Argentine people felt a deep resentment toward foreigners especially in light of the facts: they live so far away, they have fought against the British only recently, their values are simple having family at the top, and that they have been so deeply oppressed by their own governments that they don't see any reason for other countries to care.

The British had left their influences in Argentina to be sure, the main old rustic train line into the city was definitely a living example of English history. Polo, the sport of kings, was heavily represented. Never dare even make reference to the Falklands. That is the f-word as far as Argentina is concerned.

The Argentine's have given up on caring themselves about their own form of democracy especially since they have for so long been downtrodden by fear, and punishment by their own representatives. This inner sadness is very apparent to the Argentines, and when some that Shirley met along the way during her stay in Buenos Aires questioned her one of the first things they would bring up is, "What are you doing here?" These would not be words of polite curiosity, they would be expressed through a tone of credulousness. Shirley would not know how to respond. She took it as a personal affront that these strangers would turn their shoulders away from her so coldly. It wasn't in her nature to give people scorn so when it was shown toward her, she did not in the least like the bitter feeling it left.

This conundrum would continue to baffle her throughout the two years that she lived there. It wasn't a need to be righteous, but it was natural to want to care about how others felt that really got to her in a manner that baffled her inner sensitivities. Sometimes it was outright frustrating. That inner dialogue would contend, "Why weren't people willing to go above their own grief damn it?"

She had not been properly poised for the emergence into the world that Argentina had opened her eyes to. She was absolutely dumb founded by the events that had lead her to step on to that particular airplane.

Only six short months before she embarked, she had met Leo Horatio. Their bond was instant, she responded to him from the tips of her toes, to her pupils, he was indeed a fascinating young chatter-box of a man. It was as if Leo could express everything that she had wanted to, but without any sort of dialogue between them.

There she was working in her freshly pressed uniform at the Waterford; stepping on to the locked elevator to stop on every one of the twenty floors to clear away the delicate china. Leo was new to the department, and she had no idea that there would be a new trainee on duty that day. This was a girl that was well respected by her colleagues and what was also so striking about her was the way in which she stood. Shirley was elegant in her gait; her eyes were a deep mysterious green with golden speckles which she used to look straight into another person's soul. A lot of people had commented that upon first meeting her they were for the most part, taken aback by her intensity. This intense essence was not something that she had practiced, nor was it something that she had contrived, it just was.

Leo was immediately alight by Shirley's energy and using his clever wit he talked to her on that day with such a natural agility that it was as if they were enmeshed in more than just light entertaining delightful conversation. It was a conversation to be remembered for years into the future, yet the topics were random and utterly frivolous.

Leo immediately bellowed out about T*he Young and the Restless*, and having been a big fan of the program throughout her years at university, Shirley chimed in. The two of them harped about Victor, and how many times he had come back to life. How about Nicolas, and Victoria who were only about eight years old, but suddenly over the weekend they were replaced by two teenagers. Shirley thought that it was cruel for Tracy to have to be ripped to shreds by Lauren just because of her weight, but the old victim act was becoming so stale. Leo liked Lauren who it was rumored actually would not sleep on her side for fear of getting wrinkles.

The arduous task at hand had slipped away from the two of them. They were living in a vacuum of triviality that had somehow brought them together as close as she had ever felt toward any other human being. Shirley's romantic fancies had never imagined a point of contact that stimulated her very being by such triviality. This meeting was more significant to her than any other meeting she had had in her life thus far. It was a lonely isolated existence for her until she became close to Leo. The darkness of her cloudy inconsistent relationships of the past dissolved on the day she met him in the elevator at the Waterford Centre Hotel.

Leo was different from Shirley because he had not recognized the total weight of that moment. His agenda was already spread out in front of him. He was from a privileged upper class family from the splendid Shaughnessy area of Vancouver. He had struggled to fit the mold of his Catholic upbringing, having only in his early twenties come to terms with his homosexuality.

Leo acted as if he felt the need to overcompensate for this anomaly at least when it came to presenting himself amongst the people who his high profile father associated with. The social circles that his parents ran in were ones that could not possibly be open to the prospect of a gay family member. It would have been unheard of for a conservative leaning actively political man to be proud of his out-of-the-closet homosexual son.

This was a time of great modernity, but Leo had read the signs all around him and presumed that this was a stain on the family. In fact, he had imprinted in his mind what type of response he would receive were he to proclaim his sexual preference. The presumption played out in his mind so many times that he was certain that it was part of reality.

Really his repression was the prison that he had put himself in. The reasons were completely illogical in light of what his family had offered to him in his life where there was never a doubt that humour and love had been consistently around him. Leo's parents were from an era when sociological issues were new forms of enlightenment, however much they permeated their day to day existence in a minimal fashion. Leo was sure that he was protecting himself and them from something that they would scorn him for, perhaps as well they would blame themselves. This insecurity was deep within Leo himself, and really had no base in reality.

There were statements made in jest by several of his family members, or in disregard that were thrown around by his father, but these were superficial whims. Leo was affected by the fears of his own creation. It was an early stage in his life as a young man when he had met Shirley; he was a bundle of nerves but somehow her presence, her beauty and her eloquence had captured his admiration. He was duly enraptured by her honest appraisal of him.

The fear stood aside for the first while in the friendship. Shirley knew only the crispness of the moments, and how again they rang through her senses as such novel yet fantastically ecstatic rhythms of being. There was so little that needed to be said, and so much that needed to be put into action. Not the boorish type of exaggerated actions that people only do because they are told through long since forgotten traditions.

The traditions that were certain to have meaning were the ones that made the most sense to continue to participate in. There was a strong belief system at play within Shirley from her humble upbringing. She would feel scorn at the possibility of never entering into the vows of matrimony. There was a little girl within her that was hungering for rescue. The more that she participated in the new found world however, the more this vision of a sentinel who guided her every movement, and who protected her well-being was vanishing amongst the panoramic scenery.

This was the shifting life that she was rolling along with, sometimes not so sure of foot. Leo Horatio was bursting full of viewpoints, lessons, knowledge, and pure glee.

She knew that Leo preferred men in a sexual way but she didn't give serious thoughts as to how that would affect their relationship. The relationship did not exist as an entity, one just knew that whatever the pink elephant in the room was that loomed there due to what society dictated; it didn't matter in the moment, but sometimes certainly in the afterglow.

People are full of nuances, that of their own creations, and those that can actually be sensed. This companionship felt effervescent while at the same time other-worldly. There had been a hole in Shirley's heart which was trampled on by one very tall, and lazy boy that she went to university with. There was a period of four years that had passed since this brief glimmer of love in her life.

The passion that she had felt at the time was hot, and it fizzled out like a shooting star. The pain of this loss had burned deep within. She did not feel worthy of someone who could take the place of this desire. The issues that she had carried on her back like a two tonne brick since her childhood, were burst open once again by this, her first love. He had made his proclamation of love to her, and then shortly thereafter, cut her off at the knees by refusing to talk to her. She had ran into him by chance, and was actually given closure when he told her how sorry he was for the way he had dealt with the situation. She had felt better about this heart ache, but still could not forget how it felt to be surrounded by this overwhelmingly beautiful feeling.

Leo personified the cure to her longing to feel once again how it felt to be enthralled with someone. The passion was effortless just like a long breath from the pit of the stomach. It wasn't in the sexual sense at all, but nevertheless, it was a wonderful feeling. When her stomach would fill up with flutters of waves at the very thought of Leo, she would try to drown them out, and deny their source. She equivocated that to be intoxicated in the presence of Leo was to be intoxicated with love. She was afraid of what was happening to her on the one hand, but on the other hand she was enjoying every moment.

This fear that something could happen that would blow the entire truth out into the light and to have feelings shattered did not seem to be a possibility. When sex is not part of the equation there is less ego out there to be exposed, and therefore crushed. A bruised ego is an infuriating jarring cramp in the body. Our egos undergo such elation that is then deflated into the worst bitterness that an individual can bring into the depths of the mind. The powerful messages that seethe through one's mind affect every decision, every movement that we make.

Women and men enter into monogamous relationships without really being able to predict how each will fulfill their roles. Because of the restrictions, and pressures of marriage, and of sharing one life with one person, the choices are minimized, and the free will is stifled by concerns for that other being, and all the people that raised him. A man becomes restless after the initial sexual rushes he feels when he engages physically with his woman. A man in love with a woman, puts her on a pedestal high up above the earth. His fantasies are deviant from the woman's invariable nature. This is a young, and foolish man, who becomes attached to the idea of what a woman should be. The woman then shows herself as her nature dictates, and that is when the man loses his interest in her. He refuses to change his ideals, and the sexual part of the relationship dwindles.

She had been witness to the cold facts of the way that men relate to sex, and her true nature. The disillusionment had forced her to expand her mind about love, and romance. When Shirley's mind searched for the meaning behind the feelings that she cherished for Leo, above any other man, she could only justify them as maybe being inappropriate at times, but at other times, she had a difficult time ebbing the tide; they were like a force of nature.

The first three months of the fellowship between Leo, and Shirley were poetic, fun, romantic, and memorable. Leo took her under his wing, and showed her all of the best places to see, in and around, Vancouver. She met his family at a lavish dinner made by his Northern Italian mother Florencia, who pulled out all of the best china, and showed her impeccable culinary skills. Leo's father, Louis, put her in a place of honour by being insistent on having her sit right beside him, and through fits of laughter, and a barrage of interesting topics, continually poured wine into her glass. Leo's parents could not have been more pleased to have met any of his friends.

There was an instant admiration on their part, just as there had been with their son. This whimsical young woman fit right in with their family, so much so, and not only that, she presented herself in such a beautiful manner. She had passed through an open door, she had surpassed all expectations. There was an elemental ease that she possessed, which was brimming with truth. She did not have to try at winning people over, so she never did that. There were many occasions in her life, when naturally, she would zone out on conversations with new acquaintances, if there seemed to be no point to knowing them.

Leo's parents were bowled over by her emotional intelligence. She was a true road warrior with many scars that she had to bear from a very young age, but she didn't show it in her demeanor. She was pure of heart. Louis was a shrewd business man yet he could see that all of the trappings that Leo had to offer did not impress Shirley. This was a girl who could shop at the cheapest stores for clothes, and dress better than any wealthy woman. She was a refreshing change for his son. She saw through all of the material things that Leo had, and took an interest in what he was as a person.

Face value was not something that Leo had been accustomed to in his privileged existence. Even though Louis had tried to show his children that there were more important things in life than just money; he felt that he had failed to resonate that enough. He had tried; he had made sure that Leo attended a good university, and had always provided for him. Though he could have spoiled his son by buying him an expensive car, he chose instead to provide modest material things to instill in him a good sense of values. Here was a girl that pleased Louis because he knew she wasn't there for the privileges that Leo could bring. Shirley's mere presence added something that did not have a price attached to it. Her soul sprang from the confusion, and complexity of daily life. There was a tone in her voice that conveyed what she wanted to express, that others adored.

She had never felt as giddy with the men that she had romantic feelings for, as she did when she was with Leo. It really did not make practical sense. It was an anomaly to the drone undertone that people who live in a regulated society, are complacent about. The two of them would complete each others' sentences with a fit of laughter. These laughing attacks were annoying to some people, who would only give the pair a strange look, and then proceed to avoid them.

Sharon felt a pang of jealousy when she saw Shirley driving around with Leo in his VW Rabbit convertible one day, on the way to the hotel. They seemed to be on this permanent vacation when they were together. Off in their own little pleasurable world. Sharon had not seen her friend for nearly a month at the time that Leo started working at the hotel. It was not in Shirley's character to ignore anyone, especially Sharon, who had been so supportive of her. I

It seemed very apparent to Sharon, that Shirley, had been transformed by Leo's presence. There was something insincere about the way that Leo controlled her friend. She was under some kind of magic spell, of note, were the topics that she was suddenly interested in, and the drastic hair cut that she floated into the hallway with one day. It was a complete make over. This new outer appearance was reflective of the link between Shirley, and her new partner in crime. This was how she viewed it, but others who had encouraged their friend to be free, knew the young man was just biding his time, knowing full well the affect he had on this vulnerable shell of a woman.

Sharon was loyal, and knew that this would be a phase that Shirley would grow out of. Her feeling right off the bat was that Leo was one itchy kind of princess. Her precious friend was a very special person, who could forgo people's faults, she was accepting of compromise. This was the beginning of the control that Leo had on Shirley. He saw his position with her in that first month, very clearly. He knew that she would go to the ends of the earth for him, if she was able to.

There was a sense of infinity to their union. It wasn't as strong a feeling as Leo knew that Shirley had felt for him, but in some strange way he needed her, and this permeating insincerity was as a result of his own self hatred. That, if let loose, could certainly crush another spirit.

After three months of working at the Waterford Centre Hotel, and knowing that his destiny was not to be tied to either a heterosexual woman, nor to working in a subservient position of employment, Leo announced very suddenly to her that he would be flying to London England in one week's time. Due to the shockingly dramatic way that Leo had made his announcement, and to the amount of one on one time that they had spent together, Shirley felt devastated by the news.

There was a lump in her throat that caused her to stop breathing for a moment in time. Leo had explained in a matter of fact manner, that he would be living with his sister, and would be traveling all around Europe for an undetermined amount of time, for years in fact. Leo wasn't certain, but he knew that he had a perfect opportunity to see the world, he had a sister that he felt very close to who could provide a place for him to stay, and he didn't need to worry about money, not right away.

London, England would be the perfect place to be, to start a fantastic career. After all, Europe had so much to offer to Leo, he was barely in his twenties, and he wasn't any where near thinking about settling down anywhere. Europe was a dream destination for any young Canadian man. There were so many cultures, and so many countries in the vicinity. Leo was ecstatic with his decision, and with his luck had a place to stay.

Shirley vacillated between being numb, to being active, in any way that she could, so that she wouldn't have to bear the thought of not having Leo living in the same city, let alone the same continent. Her beautiful apartment in Kitsilano, her other friends, and her secure job were not enough to bring her comfort in the days after he left.

She did not see that the tearing motion that this separation had in her mind, was something that she should have paid closer attention to. It was a battle for her to admit to the fact that she was intoxicated by this strange arrangement. She was being set up like a lamb to a slaughter house. She found herself at the end of some strange situations, when she hit several litres of wine in one sitting, or when she would end up laying in bed beside a crazy bellman, after a forgetful night of debauchery.

It was really hard to believe that she had been so affected by one person. The element of thought control had never occurred to her because she just pursued trying to be numb. It couldn't possibly be that someone like Leo could be so selfish. There were times when she would wander on to the beach on hot sunny days by herself and hear Pink Floyd's "Wish You Were Here," play on someone's radio as she wrote it in a letter to Leo, and let herself get carried away in the very thought processes that involved him. It was difficult to forget about him even though she tried so many times, and when she was on the brink of feeling better after months of not hearing from him, in an instant, she would be drawn in again by some outrageously romantic gesture on Leo's part.

In one instance, she received a box of chocolates from Belgium from him. They were all broken to bits but the package came with pages, and pages of letters that he had written for her, detailing his adventures. This really wasn't what Leo had on his agenda to make Shirley important in his life; at least not as important as Shirley had lead herself to believe.

She was coming from a very different insecure emotional chaos. Their fellowship was only strengthened by the long separation as Shirley resolved to live the situation. It was after one year and two months after Leo had departed that she decided to get on an airplane to Europe. This impulse was not really intended solely toward the end to see Leo. The feelings by then had waned in her mind. She had met a new friend who was straight from France who urged her to get over, and see all of the things that she had studied about, and had admired. There hadn't been many letters from Leo in recent months at that time, but there was a pull for her that she could not deny to get over to the European continent.

The idea did not initiate with the prime directive being to visit with Leo, it just so happened that she had received a phone call after she had reserved her flight that would bring her to Paris. The trip was really meant to be a time for her to visit with her French friend Sophie with whom she had shown great kindness towards while she was a nanny in Vancouver, and who with reciprocity had promised her the time of her life along the country side in the South of France.

Shirley jumped at the opportunity, her impulses had taken on a heightened reality, and she didn't pause for one second when she met the elderly man who gave her the one on one detailed attention when she booked the flight. The flight arrangements were made on a date that had no significance to her at all it was just a date that she literally pointed her finger to on the calendar, October 26, 1995.

Leo came swooping into Shirley's life again after a long silent absence. He chirped with excitement at the prospect of seeing his friend in France, and showing her around. Here was a well seasoned traveler who knew he had made a distinctly unique connection. Leo was truly disillusioned by his job arrangements in London, England. There were many promises in sales, there were outrageously expensive dives to live in, and there was his retail job at Convent Garden Market. This was something that he could not get his head around, the toil it took to live, and survive in London. He was used to the comfort of his life in Vancouver, and not the barrier that was brought on by the stiff class system in England.

There he hadn't a hope in a million to make the proper connections. Even with the proper connections it was old established upper crust people that truly made a good living in

London. Being young and taking advantage of his time over in England because of its location was what he had to do. It was a way to stay sane, so he took a French immersion course in France while Shirley with serendipity had just decided to land in France first.

The instant she landed in France she was free of all her sorrow and fears. Leo was never far from her spiritually, but this was a chance to experience first hand together all that the two of them had studied in university only five years before. France was incredible. There were really no words that could describe the feelings that this essentially studious girl had when she landed in Paris.

Leo had arranged to meet her at the train station in Marseille from which point they would whisk away to Aux En Provence. This was the most beautiful countryside in all of France. She could not help feeling like she was in some surreal painting. She had packed absolutely perfectly for the three weeks the two of them would travel by rail, and stay at the modestly priced pensions, and small hotels.

The two of them would go through France, Spain, Belgium, and Holland. There were miles of laughter, wine, tours, and museums that they would conquer side by side. It was poignant that the very first stop on the tour was in Nimes where they lunched in the park with wine and baguettes. There was so much for them to talk about that the hours zoomed by with Shirley's heart brimming with more love in the moments of new experiences that sped by.

Due to the fact Leo was a very selfish young man he had disparaging thoughts about how he would be able to stand spending every moment of three weeks with another person, and still be able to feel that he was not being smothered. Shirley knew how to fulfill the hours that they had together without having to make either compromise in any way. There was an innate selfless quality to her character that she was not bothered by going along with any plans that others had made. For the duration of the trip, there wasn't any discussion of what the other person wanted to do in opposition to the other. This was something that she would have to learn later on in her life. This was a moment in her life when time was of no consequence. She knew how to live in the here, and now. She was not fettered by regrets; there was no need to worry about anything that was purely inconsequential.

She would listen to others complain about things, and not be able to empathize for the pain they felt that they were enduring. It seemed as if there never was a need to complain. One could easily replace complaining by hurt up until that point in life. Everything that had gone wrong with the world must somehow be the consequence of Shirley's actions. It somehow seemed logical that it would be easier to be at fault than to risk having others turn against her.

This accountability for the actions of others was a completely heavy weight for any young woman to bear. It would come out in the form of binge drinking, keeping extremely physically active, or just through isolating tears. There were so many instances where she truly was alone. These fears were real that if anything tragic were to happen to her it may be hours, or days before anyone would notice. There were excruciating sleeping binges where for three days she would not even get dressed, nor eat, or even want to present herself to the world of living people. This sorrow came from the loneliness of her childhood. If the childhood that Shirley experienced were anyone else' fault than it may have been a much quicker process in order for her to pinpoint how to think differently in order to conquer her fears.

There was no one source for the fear. Each day in life was meant as a discovery of how to overcome the obstacles. It was so difficult for her particularly to even know what the obstacles were. So when it came right down to it, if there were some sort of attitude adjustment that needed to occur for her it would be incumbent that she was more than willing to bend her will.

The destructive nature that she was in natural possession of compelled her to go through the dreaded paths when in life that one makes decisions that were not necessarily for the best. Mistakes were a give-in for a young woman like Shirley, who was really discovering her foibles; in not the most head-on of fashions. What seemed to be so important to her one day, would suddenly buckle under the whims of the moments. These were problems that were two-fold one of being indecisive, and the other being not a sufficient enough judge of character.

There were moments that she could single out in her memory and vanquish that person she was so bent on becoming. That person would face herself in the mirror the next morning, and find herself in a moment of despair one that had no possibility of washing away but in a pool of tears.

So it was that the process of bullying never seemed to get easier. It was upon her mid-20s that she learned not to bully herself anymore. It was an identity struggle that for some lasts decades, but Shirley had not even reached the point of recognition. If Leo wanted her to throw away a pair of shoes because he thought they were vulgar, then so be it. It was difficult to make a final decision of who you wanted to be. It had occurred to her, why would anyone want to put a definition to themselves. Wasn't it fair to say that life was ever-evolving and who wouldn't want to evolve? The shoes were not who Shirley was.

These things that represent us in moments of pain that we wear, or that we say, only serve us for a flash in the pan. The integral private fears and the pain of living are really what Shirley learned to put at the top of her brain. She knew that she did not have to be sorry for being confused. Leo had made her feel as though she were wrong to have doubts, or not to take a hard line about everything.

Life, as she knew it, was not meant to be full of hard lines. This is the wisdom that Shirley with all of her confusion, and her soft lines brought forward to her friends. Her true friends knew instinctively that the soft lines were the gifts that she had to give to the hard world. Every moment that she would lay in her bed in pain, she would say to herself either out loud, or in her head, that she would not change.

The pain of depression was insidiously present, yet it wouldn't need to be hidden. Caring deeply about others although it was a painful experience most of the time, was the only thing that she knew. Every one mattered. There was a synergy amongst people that she recognized, a oneness, so to speak. When she was a very young girl of seven, she remembered being tortured about her own genetic makeup, the fact that she wasn't born with blonde silky hair.

Every depiction on television, in magazines, and even as reflected by Barbie dolls of the mid-1970s showed that the ideal beauty was a tall blonde woman who was overtly sexy. The sex part was something that Shirley was not in tune with at such an early age, but the message that she was hearing loud and clear was that blondes were more feminine, and more sought after. It was depicted that the most popular girls were blondes whose hair was long and silky.

She was most obviously not a fair haired girl, nor was her hair silky. The texture of her hair was like steel wool. The tangles were mangled into her skull. As a young girl she struggled with the natural frizzy hair that she could do nothing to tame. There were such a myriad of products that were on the market at the time, even one that dared to name itself as a verb, to soothe that wild beastly hair. That beast could not be tamed. She had developed through several nucleus revelations in her lifetime. Even at this primal stage in her existence, she remembered feeling trapped by the circumstances of her being. It was also a time in her life that she was confused but the oneness of humanity. If people were at the end of the day all the same why were there so many societal divisions?

Even at this young tender stage in her life Shirley felt hopeless. The experience of not having control over the colour of her hair and eyes, or the freckles on her skin, and the silly alignment of her teeth. This was an emotion that welled up within her even at the age of seven. There was the ideation of suicide that would haunt her like a living nightmare during the seconds before she would sleep at night. This was pure self degradation even before there could even be a sense of wonderment.

Her home was so volatile that she remembered her viewpoints through the first friendships she had with other girls of her age. They seem to have had a special language with their mother's who spoke to them in sing- song phrases. Shirley thought that all grown ups were out to expose her for the fiend that she really thought she was. No one was there to reassure, to tell her any thing different. There existed so little time for discussions, or for questions.

To be reticent was a way to stay away from the flame. Rage was an emotion that was just below the surface. This was the type of modeling that was taking place in right in her home. The social disparities that were apparent from one's early inside life were detected by her sensibilities from the time that she was three. The economic disparities came as silent revolutions to her shortly after that.

Three: There Must Be Some Way Out of Here

Words of Valor: Remember the things that you first came to know.
Take education very seriously, you can't back
down from time.
Don't be afraid to form an opinion.

Going to church every Sunday had its rewards. A luxurious item would be bought specifically for going to hear from the gospel according to those young guys, the holy apostles. Jesus wasn't the only one who knew what he was talking about. There were twelve other faithful followers who hung on every word that he said. Some of these fellows were quiet congenial, and full of fresh perspectives. To Shirley, Jesus seemed like an easy going kind of leader. He forgave everyone, he helped people, and he led a very free lifestyle as signified by that burlap sack, rope belt, and his famous one strapped sandals. Though her malleable brain couldn't exactly capture the complex concepts that she heard, and read about, they certainly seemed to be very practical ones. That Jesus guy seemed so young, and full of an honest, quiet, peaceful wisdom.

She learned through her early indoctrination to Christianity, that the wisest people were the ones who didn't have to expose themselves to people. Humility is what built strong communities.

Quiet, strong, humble people were spread amongst the feeble minded, to aid them. This was an important value to her, that she had expunged from early study of biblical dialogues.

She had formed an early opinion about God, the Father, who had his own original book, and his was the first. He seemed relentless in his power. This was a durable character that would be fierce in the face of those who did not obey. According to what she was taught, the Father was frustrated because, he spent thousands of years before his son Jesus was born trying to get people to listen to him. Humanity was unruly before Jesus came along. Disobedience towards the Father meant that we all had to be tormented for our sins whether we did anything or not. Yes, the Father or God as he was sometimes called, did speak through clouds, thunder, and lightning every time.

The part about humans being born with the sins of our father's – fathers were accepted at Church. As an apostle, your duty was to obey the rules set out not only by the Father, but also by Jesus, without question. While the Father punished everyone, and said that everyone was a sinner at birth; Jesus was completely different.

According to what Shirley understood in all of those early years of going to church, and studying the Bible, was that she was a little scared about learning these philosophically, unsound historical stories. There was another part of the God family that she wasn't quite sure about, who was the cause of the fear in her mind. This was the third part of the trinity, the Holy Spirit guy, who only appeared maybe once in that huge book, and his character seemed insignificant, yet highly significant at the same time. Her mind couldn't quite wrap around the spirits' creepy story, and it didn't make any sense except to be scary.

She was raised with popular media like the movie, '*The Exorcist*', which was a huge sensation amongst critics, and audiences for shock value, in 1973. The remembrance came back of the first time she heard this faction of the family referred to as, the Holy Ghost, in prayers. Her ears perked up,..."In the name of the Father, and of the Son and of the Holy Ghost. Amen." This white sheet dangling in the air popped into her imaginary world, and this was part of the immediate God family? Church in a nutshell, was frightening to the young Shirley.

Priests wore these long formal white dresses that had some Elvis-like sleeves, and embroidery on them. Elvis even seemed obscure to her as a little girl too, how odd it seemed that a man would wear his hair in such a by-gone era style and belt out huge anthems while jiggling around on his tip toes. The early 70s were warped! The church mass was in reality one hour, sometimes it went on for longer. The kneeling, the standing up, the kneeling,..."He died and was buried. On the third day he rose again." This was some heavy adult concepts that were being drilled into such young minds whose brains hadn't even begun to develop.

She remembered walking through St. Peter's Cemetery during

the Stations of the Cross at Easter while the ground was still frozen, and the trees were barren. It was a desolate, violent, painful, and truly adult-like pilgrimage, that had an indelible affect on her. The thought did occur that those adults sure did partake in some crazy stuff as a hobby. The procession walked slowly throughout the cemetery while they stopped every few hundred feet to glare up at the statues of this young man in pain; he was defeated, bloody, and full of sweat. How indignant could people make other people be? This was gruesome, and oh so tiresome, for a ten year old. She knew that she did not want to have to participate in something like that again in her lifetime. How dreary to have to follow a crowd of people around a cold, wet and pot-holed cemetery just to see intimately how excruciating it was for this Jesus guy to die a very slow, tortuous death.

The upside to church was the music, and there was always fresh flowers amongst a beautiful art display on the stage. The priest stood upon his pulpit miles away from the congregation. This very young girl thought the whole service so bizarre, and why did this priest have a microphone? Jesus wouldn't have had a microphone back in the day. The priest talked incessantly about something very personal, something beyond the scope of a little girl, and about the congregation giving him more money. It was as if he wouldn't be able to survive on such an impoverished salary. The insincerity was palpable. The reality was that there were no taxes to pay. Then there was a real sense of community in the formalities when everyone shook hands with each other.

She would display her beauty with the fine clothes she was given to wear in that nice building. However, Shirley was happy when the final moments would finally arrive. She was naturally drawn to the fact that there were some churches that were more beautiful, and that had angels floating in the sky. These angels looked like the most beautiful, and harmless of all beings that were associated with the church. The little angels didn't speak, they just hovered around people playing very beautifully carved instruments, on the other hand, the older angels were a serious enterprise. They looked weary, and old.

Gabriel was the man with the briefcase who would knock on your front door with a neatly wrapped package, and seemed like he was just as feminine, as he was masculine. Gabriel possessed that tranquil quality to him that Shirley had been attracted to from the earliest moments of her life. These were humans who assessed their environment; they listened intently. The sage-like qualities arrested her attention. It was as though these types of people were listening to a universal dialogue that no one else could hear.

At a young age, she thoroughly recognized the inner qualities that people had, who passed through her life. The recognition could be drowned out by a lot of other white noise; however there was a special power that she possessed in her memory. The sins of everyone who moved through her past resonated into her life at some point along her daily journey. It was not as though she was searching for the ghosts, and their remnants, they just naturally followed her because of her strong memory.

After mass was over, it was a time to enjoy the bountiful pleasures that only an invention such as, ice cream could bring. A little girl with a giant ice cream from Shaw's Dairy Dell was a sight to behold. She would completely immerse herself in the process that this Sunday ritual was responsible for. Mass was painful indeed, the songs sounded so insincere and the choir was trying to out do the priest. Only God was supposed to be front, and centre at church. This parish had increased because the mass had become increasingly about the music. The priest was outraged by the choir who were full of bright modern ideas, and talent. The priest wanted to simplify the proceedings, to make them less flashy, and to silence the passion that each of the apostles had.

The priest wasn't even aware that he was actually pushing the faithful people away. Amid controversy, the church still lingered on. Shirley's father held on to the church with his very soul. He had become bankrupt in every way to the point of no return. She learned through her father that sometimes the lessons that life has to offer us are the ones that should not be put off. He was a gambling man in every sense of the word. Gideon Raymond was the head of a very large, and God fearing family. He had been the third of eight in his impoverished family. The church had provided refuge and community for Gideon's family.

In return for the church's support, Gideon grew up to strictly adhere to God the Father's rules. Gideon also denied that there were many things in his environment that he could not control. Denial was second nature to the whole of the brood that he raised under his tight fist. Such as were the strict rules of his time, Gideon would take out the belt to punish his young sons for their transgressions. His daughters lived in constant fear of being discovered with cigarettes, or wearing make-up, or other such coming of age rituals.

Shirley would spend her youngest years in the shadow of all of the controversy between her twelve siblings. It wasn't that she was sheltered from any of the tempestuous struggles; it was just that she was much too young to participate. None of the girls in the family were close to her age. Shirley was surrounded by her brothers who were closest in age to her.

It was like winning the lottery as far as family order were concerned. The baby of the family has certain privileges. Being too small to cause trouble during the twilight of her father's life also had its benefits. There was only one time that Shirley was scolded, and smacked on the behind. It was a very hot day in the projects where she grew up. The sun was beating down on her as it did every day that she would go to the public pool. The line-up would start a half an hour before it opened every day. She would spend the entire day at that pool. Later she would go home, and be so desperately hungry that any food would do.

It was a special day indeed that she had the awareness that

Gideon had stashed a bag of oranges in his filing cabinet. She raced into her parents' room, and stole one. She was cognizant that if she were discovered she would most certainly have to pay the dire consequences. Rosemary, her mother, caught her daughter stealing the orange right out of her bedroom, and was fuming from the complete disregard that her daughter had shown. Shirley ate her reward in a field away from the house, but she could see from the bushes that the entire neighbourhood were searching for her. It didn't matter to her whether or not she would be in a world of trouble for her actions. The sweet juicy orange that she had barely ever had in her life was well worth the penalty. The neighbours apprehended her like a fugitive after hours of her being crouched under a bush watching as people called her name.

Gideon was beside himself with the task that he now had on hand. This man in his early 50s the head of a very large family who worked all day selling cars, now had to formally punish his 6 year old daughter for stealing an orange. It was with regret that he lashed into her back side, and she cried but she truly did not feel remorse. This was a heavy lesson for such a small girl.

Sometimes there are actions that one must take in life to reap rewards, but at the same time the rewards come with a price. The rigors of being flanked by young boys would sometimes cause a bit of wear, and tear on the young girl. Naturally, she was at an age when she modeling her behaviour; one day when she climbed a wire fence. The wire got caught on her elbow on the jump down.

The cut was so deep that she had to be rushed to the hospital where she was given stitches. In some strange way, the trip to the hospital was welcome to the young girl. Her mother was absent for most of her tribulations, but in this instance, her mother was there. Rosemary, the beautiful gentle soul, who was vulnerable to the strict fraternal influences of the society that she grew up in. Shirley reveled in the attention, no matter what the circumstance.

When children are young and living in groups they seem to be like terrific germ factories. Shirley was not exempt from the spread of the measles, nor the chicken pox which spread like wild fire in her household. The measles were especially excruciating. At just five years of age, she was asleep for days, and her fever had spiked to such a high temperature that she remembered seeing Barbie dolls dancing on the curtain rod. She was so weak that she could hardly move, but she found it hard to resist just getting up from that bed and playing with her joyful dancing delusions. It wasn't a scary delusion at all; as the dolls were dancing around having fun. There must have been a great compulsion in the little girl to have one of those beautiful dolls.

Dolls were a very rare commodity for the children of the Raymond family. There was one Christmas morning that she was awakened by her brothers at four in the morning just so they could see what the big package under the tree was. She opened the box to find a doll about the size of her self, who not only walked and talked, but she also roller skated. The doll's voice boomed out of the loud speaker in its back, "Let's go to the park!" At precisely the right timing Shirley and the boys heard Gideon chime in, "We're not going to the park at this time in the morning!" The roar of their father's voice was enough to send the little children scurrying away like mice.

Gideon had provided for his large family the best way that he knew how. He had given up on drinking for five years, but his dreams for the future would never be realized. Gideon died suddenly leaving a house full of children, a distraught, overwrought wife, and debt.

On that first night in June, Gideon tried to fight back from the aeortal aneurism, but lost his life. The news spread so very quickly to all of the children who were sleeping at home, but knew that their father was in serious danger. Earlier in the day, Gideon had walked slowly into an ambulance having complained for two days about lower back pain. He had become progressively weaker in the days proceeding. In looking back with shock she remembered that the last thing he did, was give her a quarter to go and buy herself a popsicle. That was amazing because that one quarter was worth five popsicles. Gideon had made his last kind gesture toward his youngest 8 year old daughter. She then remembered not being awakened by anything that fateful night, except for the sounds of sobbing. The entire family had gathered, all except for the eldest son, who was living on the west coast.

All were in various stages of mourning. Some were sobbing

loudly; others were having hushed discussions, while Rosemary was frozen on the couch asking for a cigarette. Shirley's life had changed in an instant. The complete ramifications of her father's death, would present themselves to her through years, and years of change. Gideon had a huge personality for which he was famous for. The laughter, and the wit, with which all of his children were blessed, were what gave her strength, when there was no doubt, that she felt weak. Life was broken for many people on the night Gideon died so suddenly.

His presence reverberated in every inch of his house, and his character stood on its own long after he stopped breathing. Shirley, and her brothers were urged to write a letter to their father so that he could bring it with him into his grave. She didn't remember exactly what she wrote, but at such a young age she knew what sorrow was. Walking by the open casket, she slipped the letter in his breast pocket, and touched his frozen cold face. Those bright blue eyes were closed, and Gideon looked so good. It is a strange, reoccurring experience at a funeral, when people comment that the dead person looks good. It's as though the mourners are at a loss of what to say. It was true that Gideon looked good. This final glimpse at the person was meant to leave a positive impression. No one would want to walk past a casket of a person who didn't even look like he, or she did in life.

Gideon looked good, his face wore a tranquil expression, his hands were clasped over his chest in prayer, and he wore the most fabulous, of all of his many fabulous suits. He was a proud man, whom upon a quick impression, looked like a man of affluence. Though he had died without material wealth, he still managed to look smashing. Shirley admired her dapper father, every day when he left their broken down neighbourhood; he looked flashy, and unmistakably well put together. His entire day could be a wash out, but he still managed to present a good front. This was the type of stamina that she would integrate into her being, so that she could resist any number of disasters in her life. She knew even at the age of eight, that the lives of the many people with whom she was associated with, were worth integrating. She had the privilege of be watchful of the mistakes of those who were older, and more experienced than herself.

The world would be distinctly different in Gideon's absence. Rosemary had been overcome with the responsibilities that she now had to face. She was so tired everyday, that she couldn't function. Her mother was overcome with grief and would sit in front of the television, to bury her fears with prescribed medicine, and cigarettes. No one would drive her to school, nor would the family go to church anymore. It wasn't until two weeks had gone by that Shirley went back to school. She was afraid to tell anyone about her father's death. Father's Day was only a few days away, and the children were urged to make something in class.

She made a card that she told her mother that she would put on his grave. Rosemary burst into tears when she heard her little daughter tell her about her Father's Day card. Gideon's funeral was too expensive for the family to bear. All of the older siblings pitched in whatever they could to pay for two plots, but the stone would take a few years to be erected. Processes and decisions were always reached amongst controversial, organized chaos.

What really mattered to that little developing brain is that it seemed so wrong to leave that person who meant so much to your small world in the ground where bugs, and grass would cover your body. The person would be in the dark, and be locked up in a box. It was devastating to Shirley that death could be the end. How cruel that people have to live their existence through almost insurmountable obstacles, and then be laid indignantly in a box, under the ground. This actuality of the fascinating finality would be explored by her every year of her life. Death was almost shrouded and was a dubious topic to almost everyone, yet it was so necessary.

To her uncultured eyes some of the rituals that mourners went through were exploitative, or basically the term is; overboard. It had become such a daily reality for her, even in her 20s, that she learned that she could feel comfortable about it. It was fortunate that she had been able to deal with death from such a young age instead of delaying the inevitable. She was also able to live with the fond memories that she had of Gideon.

He wasn't this abusive addict that she had heard about. Gideon was a man who was down on his luck during those last years, but he was trying very hard to make amends. Her father could be whatever Shirley's mind wanted him to be. Thus, death can be an exalted state. People who die, are more than often, remembered for the positive deeds that they had done. It's absurd to think that people intend to gather at a funeral to spit on the grave. To mourn someone, is to embrace all the qualities that you want to remember. It was difficult for the child that Shirley was, to part with her father. She would cry about him, and curse him at times when she knew that she needed a boost.

As trite as it seems, life inevitably needed to continue. Her mind would wander through the intimacy that she had resolved that she had had, with losing a close, relevant person. Gideon was not the perfect being, no he was in sharp contrast to that, but in the end he knew what truly mattered, and that was to abide by the church in faith, and to keep his family together. Life was full of loss, and this was just one more loss that one had to bear. The feelings that she harboured toward Gideon would flow, and ebb just like the pendulum of the clock. There was a backlash of commentary from all of the family members; some were very flattering, and some, not so much, people need to work through their grief. She pieced together what this man's character stood for.

His personality outshone the amour that he wore to protect himself. The need to read which fortified her intrepid spirit, and the controversial side of the adult that she would become, had sprung from this man, and her less volatile impulses of tenderness, and love sprung from Rosemary, her mother.

Loss of the most crucial of elements to her very young life, made her very familiar with pain. It wasn't the pain. and suffering of just a few people. The pain, and suffering of many people not only physically, but especially mentally, was what she had to acquaint herself with at the spring of her essence. Somehow, she emerged from early childhood untarnished by the concept of pain.

Pain was an equalizer that made every human feel like they had actually accomplished outstanding feats at the end of the day. There was one very pernicious thing about pain, and that was it was something that entities experience on every level of the senses. Pain was a common thread that drew people towards each other in harmony. Pain was palpable, or it could make it self appear as intangible. Visions of people fighting with someone in the throes of pain, seem inappropriate. Pain was sweet, because it always was a remarkable happenstance that had an unflinching hand, in making it appear. Evaluations of pain fascinated the young girl. It had a mysterious ethereal quality to this young mind. The reactions of a person who is witnessing another in pain, were enough to warm any cold heart. A sense of reverence for a survivor of enormous pain, put a person far above the average cycles of life. Pain was extraordinary.

The voices out in society were not known to her at the time, but there was one common denominator to the whole concept, and that was that pain could occur on a regular basis, but it was never dull.

Moreover, pain was not superficial, nor was it routine. No one could be considered to have a predictable reaction to pain. She noticed that each person's version of pain was as individual as they were. There was a lot of DNA shared by the people in her immediate family, but to truly know each person, it was powerfully evident how different from one other they were. Each one completely unique.

Clearly in the case of this large family, there were drastically foreboding events that shook up some lives. This dramatic backdrop certainly made her aware that people could be damaged by, not just their actions, but also through the processes of their minds. The specific inner dialogue could be triggered by a sense of the sublime, or it could come from anger, and hate.

Shirley learned from a very young age that the most important weapon against this hateful state, that she saw personified by the elders in her family, was to be as independently resourceful as possible. Making each of her siblings relevant to her well-being was a challenge. What it really meant was that she had to go, and pursue higher education, and make her way out of the province of Ontario. There was an urgency to this decisive action that really made it difficult to plan for any eventuality.

Thousands of miles of separation had put some effective perspective upon her life. She slid into adulthood with her hockey bag full of little treasures, and moved to Vancouver. The little girl had a dream, but she was a bit fuzzy on the details of how she was going to make it happen. The dream was humble just to get a job, and make some friends.

The fact of being bitter never became too much of an issue for her. Being a young 20-something, made her unsure of who she was. Finding that person is one thing to do, but really liking that person, is another. It was shrewd to choose not want to be the type of woman who would bring a list of expectations to each relationship. Friends held the highest position in this young woman's life.

There were no alternatives to figuring out who she could be, unless it was reflected in the people that she could trust. Trust proved to be of the most rarest commodity. Shirley believed just about anything about a person who she would consider a friend. There was no middle ground for her. The scam artists came out of the wood work, like some well trained army. It was an irresistible quality to some of the people that she met in her life; that she wore her heart on her sleeve.

Born with a keen awareness, that in relations with others. there were no expectations to be made; she quickly become a target for the most contemptuous of situations. Some treacherous individuals did not care one bit what other people thought about, nor how they would feel. Each battle with these wrong type of people would make her feel as though she were shaken to the core.

It was forgivable, but it was also difficult for the few people who really did care about her to see her falter again, and again.

The head banging against the wall action can not be endured too many times before the skull must crack. So head banging became a common occurrence when she first arrived in Vancouver. The job at the hotel had brought about rigorous changes in her life. The transformations during this period were sharp, and quick. Shirley was humming at a much higher pitch from the moment that she left all of the empty people in her wake.

Four: UP A CREEK WITHOUT A PADDLE

Words of Valor: We'll never get this time again, we'll laugh, and we'll sing.
Whispers are words, that are not meant to be heard.
Dive into the promises we give, to set us free.

From a certain perspective, Buenos Aires was welcoming a version of Shirley, that she herself could not have foreseen. With a depth of knowledge to guide her; she was once again haunted by the realities of living in close quarters with a family unit. This living arrangement was absolutely uncharted territory.

Patsy was a kind person, but she had expectations about Shirley that were never discussed openly. It was vicarious she felt that she could be dismissed at any time for violations of these expectations. The concept had escaped her one hundred percent. She had acuity in so many different things, her mind worked like a busy bee, and this made her seem flighty, or unaware. The fact of the matter, was that without knowing what is expected of you; the person engaging in a close relationship with the other person doing the expecting, comes out looking like a selfish person with a negative agenda. Does this make any sense? She did not even know what agendas were.

She knew that there were movies, and plays that depicted

people in far-fetched careers, with far-fetched perfectly harmonious lives. There may have been some action occurring in these movies, such as a person might have an epiphany, and then suddenly, they would care. Relationships in real life never played themselves out that way. She had no idea what a family unit did on a daily basis. She was expected to be able to know her role, and to learn her lines. What Shirley learned during the two years that she lived in Buenos Aires, was that people can engage themselves with material things more than with each other. If they do engage with each other, it does not seem sincere, or it is at most times, forced. There was so much that she had to fight against living within a household.

The best thing she knew how to do was to escape. She needed to find a way out of the situation that she was in with her obligations in this surrogate family that she had been cohabiting with, sadly she didn't fit in.

Finding a job in Buenos Aires was no easy task. After many months of stalling, she was finally able to work in a British run primary school. It was a very 'Topsy Turvy' type of working environment. The pay scale was so low, that all of the immigration paper work that it took to land the position, did not seem to be worth it. The trade-off was that she would be spending more time outside of the house. It was without difficulty that Shirley found herself mirroring the habits of Patsy just to show that she was agreeable. She learned that the life of a person who is dependent on anything is a sad way to have to live. She was frightened that whatever she did, or did not do would somehow be seen with Patsy's scornful eyes. This was an example of a family that looked absolutely perfect on paper, but in reality had many problems. It was not in her nature to put this kind of relationship in peril. She wanted to please Patsy in her heart but her conscious self kept on resisting the confrontation. When people who are participating in closely bound relationships are not having their needs met, over time, they become bitter and resentful. She did not want to be bitter.

The social scene in Buenos Aires opened wide for her on a night when she attended an embassy cocktail party. After about four months of living a parallel existence, along with Aunt Patsy, she glided into the room of the Canadian embassy, and out of the proverbial sky, she was surrounded by a tight knit group of single, ex-patriots. There were assembled together like the board of the United Nations; Bertrand Simmons from Hamburg, Germany; Alejandro from Mexico City; Margie from New Castle, England; Claudia Eckmeier, from Denmark, and there she was, Shirley Ramona Raymond, from small town London, Ontario, Canada.

First hand, on-the-level knowledge, by forging these special friendships, gave her the perspectives that she was wide open for, at this stage in the Buenos Aires experience. She had learned from her piles of family messages, whether these messages were spoken about, or not. To drink it all in, and take a deep breath, was how it felt the moment that she met these, her friends, from Buenos Aires. There were so many philosophical beliefs being spread by this group of people.

Bert had a critical reaction to her. The words flowed from his mouth with a gentle ease, when he was in her presence. He was a confident man. This was the first time in his life he had ever met a Canadian. It had never occurred to him that the Canadian culture would be any different from the American, therefore, he was quiet impressed with her. Bert was tall, fit, and although his frame was not bulky, it certainly was muscular. Her first impression of Bert, and his well formed limbs, was that he must be a boring type of studious guy. Bert's glasses hid the perfect contours of his face. which had plains of high cheek bones, and right down to the most softly, ample, lips imaginable. To Bert, there was no use highlighting his good looks, but he preferred to derive attention from people due to his logical, and very methodical intellect.

Shirley couldn't quite identify what it was that bothered her about Bert, but later in their relationship, she realized that he built up walls around him, because he was so very soft on the inside. The soft underbelly of this man was intriguing and was exactly where she wanted to be.

It usually took some amount of time to get to know new acquaintances. Margie broke the usual code on that presupposition. Margie was loud, sometimes crude, but so utterly authentic, that through lively interactions she could not help but to welcome her imposing character. It also was a matter of no choice in the matter, of getting to know Margie; this was a creature who indeed knew how to get under your skin. She was forceful, yet immensely friendly.

To begin a friendship with this British rose, was to be hit by an electrical jolt. Margie was the heart of this circle of friends. When she wasn't teaching in the sprawling suburbs of Buenos Aires, she was frantically setting up social events. Her frantic nature revealed itself when she would smoke the long, thin menthol cigarettes to only half way, in a fury of hand movements. Margie had lived in Buenos Aires for seven years, and she had most of the things that she wanted out of life. Her late 30s had brought about some clarity to her above the roar of her active mind; she knew that she wanted to find someone who would compliment her life, and be her life partner.

With a ferocity that only Margie had access to in her soul; she decided that she was going to make a point of meeting as many people as she could. Buenos Aires' natives, known locally as Portenos, were especially either detracted by foreigners, or attracted to them. Canadians had their fans in every country, but in Argentina it seemed so strange for these North Americans to actually contribute to their society.

The true Argentines were very protective about their nationality. They saw themselves as being a very proud, yet resolutely, sad people. Shirley could hear the topics of conversations from young Argentine business men at the Canadian Embassy party. The organizers had ordered Molson Golden just for the occasion. The year was 1996, and in terms of economics; Argentina had finally stabilized its currency.

The country had bottomed out several times, and still had some rough times to recover from in recent memories. Shirley had met a Canadian who had moved there with her Argentine mother. They ran out of cash to pay her at her job, so she had to take food stamps instead. Despite hearing stories like this, some great business minds had solidified their own currency to the at par status, with the American dollar. The Argentine families which always had their feet on the ground, had much to gain through this arrangement; however, the below-the-poverty-line families had long been oppressed by their ultra, repressive government.

Shirley could spot the eternal flame of sadness that burned in the eyes, of some of her encounters with the Argentine people, that she met at social events. They had no mechanism of escape from debt, and their cost of living certainly did not come close to their salaries. She noticed that there was a killing to be made renting furniture, so for even items like that, people would be forced to go into debt.

The European people in her group, embraced her without a thought. Margie was dialing her up on a weekly basis for a social plan. Claudia had dazzled Shirley with her candid banter about what it meant to be from Denmark. The Danes were as open minded, and well educated people, that Shirley had been exposed to. The intensity of the friendships that were forming, came clearly from the rarity of them all working in Buenos Aires simultaneously.

All of them were comfortable in the city, or more so at ease than Shirley, if not simply due to the fact that the remnants of a more glorious time were so visible, and translatable to a European mind. Claudia could speak six languages, fluently, Margie's Spanish had developed in seven years to enable her to use interesting conversational skills, but full comprehension, whereas, Bert's German lilt was stupendous when mixed in with the formal Spanish. Shirley could not utter a word of Spanish, and was cursed for doing so, every time she met up with Bert. Bert would scold her like she were a two year old child. He would say in an explosive manner, "Shirley, you can not live here and not speak the language. You must try to stop speaking English right now, it is absolutely imperative. I am extremely embarrassed for you, that you are so feeble minded."

Though Bert had started the relationship with Shirley in this superior toned manner, he remarked that there was something so pure and fascinating that emanated from her pores. He had discerned through his various discourses with Shirley that she must have the most brilliant mind he had ever encountered. He relished the time he could just have a common conversation with her. Bert's tone moved very quickly from a tone of dismay at her character to one that lovingly teased her for being so essentially Canadian.

Shirley's shyness was so attractive when it came to the responses she would hear herself blurting out. When she was with him she could hear her own voice. There definitely appeared to be a special symmetry to the friendship between Bert and Shirley. She was not in awe of him at all like she was about the force of her feelings for Leo. There was some kind of chemistry percolating amongst the pair.

Alejandro was the very first Mexican that Shirley had ever met. He had the most generous smile of anyone she had remembered. The laughter that Alex could conjure up in his diaphragm sounded like the landing of a 747 jet. There is a split second light that went off in her brain, that recognized that Alex's friendship felt like a familiar warm, secure, energetic drive.

The defining moment was when the ex-pat group all traveled to Uruguay for the weekend. The hydrofoil ferry ride only took an hour and half to land on the shores of Colonia. The Rio de la Plata had one of the widest shoreline exposures to the ocean; that it looked like one very brown muddy ocean. Shirley could not disguise her disgust whenever she walked on the shores of the river. She remembered the very first day that she drove into the city with her aunt, and peered out the left side of the vehicle at the Rio de la Plata. It was the most harrowing sight that she was witness to in her sensibility. It was so brown, and not a very warm shade of brown, but rather a dull gray sort of brown. The air coming off the river smelled like stale seaweed, petroleum, and rotten fish. This river could not possibly represent the course of nature. This was a sick river. She had been very connected to the abundant natural resources so visible in Vancouver. When living around the globe one must not try to compare any two places it's pointless.

So here she was now on the ferry to Colonia with Margie, Alejandro, an American guy named Jimmy from Minnesota, Bert, and herself. Jimmy was working temporarily in Buenos Aires for AGFA, and he was such a riotous addition to the Argentina ex-pat pack. Jimmy would have a hilarious come back expression to every conversational nuance, that would make everything he said come out like some kind of comedy routine. Shirley was so relieved to meet Jimmy, and felt an affinity to her new found drinking buddy. Alejandro was the most upbeat in the crowd, and on the way, his mood set the tone for the entire weekend journey. Margie had found that she rather fancied Alejandro, thus for this weekend, she had schematically arranged the accommodations so that all would sleep in the same large dorm-like room.

The ferry ride was a drinking session. The red wine flowed out of the bottle like a fresh spring waterfall. The expressions, and the jokes came out loud and clear, from Jimmy. Alejandro, and Margie would respond to everything Jimmy would say like a perfectly tuned orchestra. Shirley was absolutely enthralled with the camaraderie that was being shared. There could not have been a more beautiful way to spend a weekend, that she could think of, up to this point in her life.

The group of them stayed in a centuries old one bedroom apartment. Shirley called first dibs on the saggy single bed in the living room. Margie wanted to wave her magic wand, and get the intimacy she longed for with Alejandro, and claimed the one bedroom as theirs to share. Jimmy was a large, and tall man so his sleeping on the couch seemed the best plan. The first night was spent at the apartment with all of them drinking beer and wine. When it came time to go to sleep, Shirley found herself surrounded by two very large men, and one very uncomfortable whiner of a German guy.

Alejandro was what one would describe as a very, big boned man. His girth was at least 50 inches wide. The party had died, when all of a sudden, Alejandro literally fell into one of the small saggy, single beds that were in the living room. Shirley promptly thereafter jumped into her coveted position. Approximately twenty minutes after all of the lights were off, there was this thunderous roar of a snore, triumphantly, screaming in the room. This snoring sound was unlike any other that Shirley had ever heard before, humming at decibels far beyond the norm. As a consequence of this noise, Shirley could hear Bert entreating Alex, "For the love of God, stop it!" She was so pleasantly entertained by this showdown, that she felt her laughter, as it sprung from the tip of her toes, to the top of her head.

On this night, she was caught off guard, with the developments that were so very carefully forming between her, and Bert. Bert managed in a very covert manner, to slip into the single bed beside her. The sexual tension was minute given purely to the situation, but what she did feel, was that the blood was flowing deep within Bert's veins. She could feel his heart pound through his chest like a locomotive engine. At the same time, Bert was holding on to visions of Shirley in his head long after they had parted company. His heart was smoldering with the sense that there must have been a majestic creator for her. She was the antithesis of any German woman that Bert had known. Her emotions were clear, authentic, and right beneath the surface. Bert wanted to relate to that flow of love. He knew that when he would decipher the meanings of what she said, that he could only draw one conclusion about her character. Bert was in awe of Shirley, who he thought was truly derived from a divine being. She was an angel.

The next day, the group breakfasted, toured museums, and ate like splendid kings. Colonia was a charming small town that was populated by humble polite people. Shirley felt a surge of love for everything Uruguay. The simplistic classic proud people of Uruguay never stopped impressing her. Not only was the place hospitable, but it happened to have the most exquisitely rustic dining venues. There was one such lunch- stop named *The Drugstore* which was set in a park along the muddy Rio de La

Plata that served the largest portion of Paella that they had the privilege of eating. The ingredients were mainly exotic fresh shell fish, and chorizo sausage, set in a juicy stew of the fluffiest saffron rice ever known to man. The presentation of this dish was like something that would be displayed in a sumptuous vacation brochure.

All meat dishes in Argentina, and Uruguay were sautéed with the outrageously lush leaves of the basil plant. The unexpected happened for Shirley in Colonia, Uruguay. They encountered the Asados which lined the streets made of a large network of wire, in the Barrio of Uruguayan women preparing a giant feast of whole chickens for their families. It was outrageously large, like the size of a city block.

Colonia was also known for its amazingly cheap bulky wool sweaters. The designs were of unmistakable Aboriginal signature style. The cost of these hefty rough and tough wool sweaters with the intricate designs were only $10 U.S. They found themselves purchasing many of them during their stays in Argentina. On the whole, Uruguay revealed itself to be a land of morally rich people who pursued a simplistic life style. The steaks that this group of travelers ate on that weekend were of the thick, and juicy variety. They were all further impressed to discover how economical Uruguay was.

Buenos Aires had its expensive strips, and its really cheap areas of commerce. There were no in-between type of commercial spaces. Shirley had poised herself for her status within this setting. It was an intricate and sometimes very grueling process to try to find a scenario where she truly felt at ease there in Argentina. With this group of ex-pats, she fit in and felt like she could be her fabulous self.

After the exhausting yet fantastic trip over to Uruguay, Shirley found herself at Bert's high-rise apartment right on Avenida Florida, where she was content to stay. The Parque el Centro was on Bert's front lawn, thus the scene was poised to reveal the love that she so richly deserved with him. The park was splendidly located on a slope. It was comprised of: a large marble war memorial for the Las Malvinas, an exalted statue of some important General, a limestone statue of a man being tempted by the devil, a 40 foot totem pole from Canada, and the giant Jacaranda trees that while in full bloom, with their enormous purple flowers, made the city smell like sweet paradise.

It was at this moment that she finally pieced together who Bert's alter ego was. He was a clean cut, sharply dressed man, who sported crispy starched shirts, under his well tailored suits. Shirley had been presented with this jeans, and preppy polo shirt wearing man. The jeans, and the polo shirt were always the same every time she saw him. She thought that Bert must be one tightly wound conservative man.

Conservative, was a suitable adjective to describe Bert, that was, until he met Shirley. Bert felt like he wanted to loosen up when he was around her. Her commentary was so accurate, and she always had a smile on her face. It occurred to Bert that it wasn't just Shirley's face that smiled, she had this way of smiling with her eyes that captivated him.

The start of relationships were like peeling away the layers of an onion. The love that revealed itself in this instance, was one that was smoldering like normal, not at all like Shirley had seen played out in the movies. She had so distanced herself from the possibility of an arrangement of love, that would also become a reality, that as was the case with Bert, she had mentally prepared herself for the rejection, far before it happened.

Bert was proud to be German, and his command of the English language had not afforded him the ability to express himself, as he really wanted to be perceived. It wasn't Shirley that was holding this love back, it was Bert. He had been raised by a very functional family, and he had a child whom he loved with all his being, with another woman. Bert's girlfriend, and his daughter still resided in Hamburg. Sabina and Lily were Bert's lucky charms. He had just finished his obligatory military service, as well as, his business degree at university when he met Sabina. They rushed head first into a passionate sexual relationship. Sabina had acted with valor when she met Bert, but their lives had taken on new directions since Bert decided that he unequivocally wanted to live in Buenos Aires.

He had a job where he made three times as much money there,

and his office would provide free living accommodations. In Hamburg, the couple had lived comfortably in an apartment. This was an exciting opportunity that Bert jumped into with a very decisive, severe action. Sabina admired Bert's conviction, but in her life she could not envision herself at the mercy of this man who was putting his career above his partner, and his child.

It was after that particular night, that Shirley spent with Bert at his amazing apartment, that she was aware of the next layer of Bert's character. Knowing that Bert resisted sex with her because he had Sabina to consider, not to mention a little girl who he would surely die for, made him all the more attractive. This dangerous element was the element that separated passionate feelings amongst sex partners.

It was odd to her that she felt a sense of relief to know that Bert was *taken*. Shirley instinctively knew that she could easily give herself to this man, but in some other time. Long after their time together her heart would whimper at the thought of his expressions, his focused eyes watching her, and the touch of his soft hands. Timing was not to not to be so kind to her.

Bert wanted Shirley to be an important part of his life in Buenos Aires, which was a fact that he unabashedly resigned himself to. Shirley was honoured to be an active participant. Whatever the feelings were between her and Bert, for some obscure reason, she knew that she was primed for any such occasion. It was not that she had braced herself, or had feared anything in Bert's presence.

She felt so comfortable that her dilemmas could be so easily solved whenever she consulted with Bert. She knew that the basis of their relationship was trust. It is poignant when two people meet, and they know from the first second that the person they just met is trustworthy. Shirley was repelled at first by Bert's covert manner, but realized that there was good reason for it. Bert protected his tender heart.

Sabina was polar opposite to Shirley in her values. She was very charmed by depth, but really couldn't see herself as someone who could rule her life that way. To be superficial was a practiced art. Sabina was magnificently superficial. She had come to Argentina with the clear intent to break things off with Bert. Sabina knew that the lifestyle that Bert had to offer was not what she had wanted for her, and her daughter. She went through the motions in Buenos Aires for a total of two weeks. It was her vacation time after all, and she had wanted to make this final step with all of her support systems in place, when she got back to Germany.

When she met Shirley, she was struck by her beauty, her incessant, nervous laughter, but also by the unwavering kindness, that she displayed right on the surface. Upon meeting Shirley for the first time, she declared that Bert did express to her, that he loved Shirley for everything that she was. Sabina wanted her to know that she had her blessing one hundred percent to take over being Bert's love. This was not a typical scenario by any means.

She was shocked, and awed by this declaration. Sabina was leaving Bert, and was returning to Germany where she knew her destiny, was what it should be.

Shirley was numb by the experience of seeing Bert in so much pain when Sabina left. The circumstances were not what Bert had planned, and at this dark moment, he felt that he wanted to lean on this angel, that he had so skillfully taken under his wing. There she was as an immediate replacement to Sabina, in his beautiful home equipped with a giant asado, an unbelievable garden of tall basil plants, and a swimming pool.

Like a dream that she had always had; there she was serving her high end cuisine, at a bar by the poolside, under the southern cross constellations in the sky.

The sky in Buenos Aires defies an accurate description. It was like standing under a: giant light blue, effervescent, multi-faceted, absolutely spherical, giant, all encompassing, bubble. This was as close as it could be described in words. The sky in Argentina is blessed. This is where the North American can see the remarkable difference between the two hemispheres. The sky over Buenos Aires is endless. The clouds appear to be far, far away, as if they are being swallowed up in its enormity. The colour of the Argentine sky was as true a baby blue, as any that has been witnessed. The Argentine flag mimicked the shade of blue in he sky.

Shirley had remembered seeing clips of film where Princess

Diana was wearing that same colour, which had made her emanate with light. She had that innate artistic sensibility, which went a long way to express itself quite elegantly. Her agile mind was drawn in immediately by the beauty of the Argentine flag. It closely manifested what it was meant to symbolize. The flag portrayed that serene quality of a relentless sky.

From the ranches of the *Las Pampas,* to the icebergs of *Tierra del Fuego,* there were so many stories that could be told by the land. The Argentines were especially in a state of shock, about what happened to their precious Islands, *Las Malvinas*. The Argentines from the working classes have a special bond with the earth beneath their feet. An impenetrable embrace, put the masses of their society all together, for the same cause. During the Dirty Wars, the disappeared had played out their lives, within the larger schematic, but a blink of an eye ago. The *Madres de los Desaparecidos,* gathered out front of the Casa Rosada, every Thursday, with their peaceful demonstrations, just to let the politicians know, that they will not forget. She had witnessed this staple of Argentine custom many times. Had seen the shame that was the brutal defeat of the *Las Malvinas*.

Many of the working class people in Argentina believed that the rest of the world had forgotten about them. Their trust had been betrayed so many times domestically, that they had a real sense of their own futile future. The mothers have not given up on their sons, and they will continue to demonstrate peacefully outside the,

Casa Rosada, until they find out what really happened to them.

Menem was the current flavour of the week, political puppet, that the Argentines had to endure. Shirley picked up on the Hello Magazine story, that showed the suspected fate of the son of Menem, who was then the President of Argentina. The glossy pictorial article detailed the questionable circumstances of his death, and it was speculated that Menem's son was thrown from a helicopter into the river.

Her awareness was raised with alarm that any conversation with an Argentine, at a cocktail party, or at any formal social function, usually ended up with a heated political discussion. She had the experience of being on the end of more than one passionate discourse, regarding the so called reverence, that the Argentine's felt toward, *Evita*. They were not giving *Evita's* legacy any credence.

As a matter of fact, most Argentine people that Shirley had discussed the topic of the dictator's young wife with, felt that she exploited the impoverished, more than anything. *Evita* was no saint as far as her people with informed viewpoints were concerned. She took away from the poor with her furs, her Haute Couture, her diamonds, and her bottle bleached, blonde locks. The photos of Evita handing out money to those that were set up in the her housing projects were mere photo opportunities, meant solely to bolster Eva Peron's public image.

After all, Eva Peron was married to as cruel a dictator as any that the Argentine people had ever witnessed though there were more than just a few. The glitz and the glamour did not whitewash the stains that the Argentine people had to bare. Evita's legacy continues to enrapture the simple religious people who need some comfort from a matriarchal figure. No matter what neighbourhood she explored in Buenos Aires, there was always a cathedral, and even at each stop on the Retiro train line, there appeared a fancy shrine, with the most decked out Mary, Mother of God, Shirley had seen yet.

The Southern Cross constellation appeared in an elongated formation, it was astonishing really. The only stars Shirley had ever seen in a clear night sky that made her take notice were when she had lived in Thunder Bay. How does one reference Thunder Bay figure on this cosmic journey? It happens because, Shirley had worked her way through high school, and was hard pressed to complete her graduation. Upon graduating, she had demonstrated only mediocre grades. The University of Western Ontario would only accept straight '*A*' student's right out of high school.

So she took the long way around, so to speak. After one very long year in Thunder Bay, she went back to London Ontario to finish her degree. This was a spring board because being away from her most stifling of pasts, had intrinsically changed her. Within the new environment, she really had a chance to test out life skills. One glimmer of hesitation would, in those years, have cost her dearly. When it came right down the heart of any matter, this wandering traveler was able to navigate herself.

Five: TREES HUGGING TREES

*Words of Valor: Desolate rebirth strengthen the soul.
Part with the ways of old, not before
understanding them.
Treat it, as is if it's going to last.*

Being in an isolated environment such as Thunder Bay had taught Shirley more about the landscape of herself. In subtle ways, the environmental landscapes around us tends to shape our fundamental lives. It was no wonder then, that Buenos Aires, was yet again another city where she could wrestle with another part of herself. In the first foray into to the living far away existence, she had to set up house with an absolute stranger named Heather, who had ulterior motives; just to have her there to pay the bills. It eventually turned out that she would end up paying for more than her fair share.

Vulnerability comes at a high cost, when it comes to finances. Especially when the people you enter into the contract with are less than trustworthy. Thus, keeping integrity seemed to be the most important factor to maintain, when one is financially weak. That first year of university was a tough one especially emotionally. She had a very limited student budget that had to last for four months. It didn't seem possible for her to get a job, where she knew no one, had to go to school full time, and didn't have transportation. The apartment was very far off campus. The public transit system was rudimentary at best. The art of compromise weighed so heavily on this young woman.

During the first two months she had struggled with the growth of four wisdom teeth, that were plaintively coming through her skin. The budget did not allow for food. She was resigned to the steady diet of Red River cereal every morning for weeks, with nothing else for the whole day. When Christmas came around that dark, cold winter, she went back into the family fray, and spent an even colder deep freeze in Ottawa. She would look back on that time as one of her most defeated, and desperate of times in her life.

Years would pass, and she would look at that photo of her and her white complexion, with hollow eyes; when she weighed under 100 pounds. It was as though all of her insecurities had come crashing through the flood gates, and all that she had feared the most had manifested.

There was a brief period during the last month of her stay up there in the far reaches of the Canadian forest, when she felt loved, and accepted. The fellow students from her classes had invited her to stay in the dorm, and that is where she stayed for the last of that school calendar year.

There were parties in every corner, of every room, and on every floor. There didn't need to be an occasion. Being a university student in Thunder Bay seemed reason enough to celebrate, night after night. For those students who were made of more substance, the constant parties were boring, but to Shirley; it was like living in a pub twenty four hours a day. There were even brief moments of extreme happiness for her during that of her last days, in Thunder Bay. When she said her final goodbyes, she had been promised by more that a few of those people, that they would always be friends.

Perhaps people say that in their youth, but somehow she had felt that their time together had meant something. For the first time in her life she was thrust into a strange environment with complete strangers, who had very little in common with her. The shyness wore off very slowly for her, as she learned to peel away the surface, which masked how it was difficult to show people who she was inside.

Drinking draft beer from a straw was the perfect elixir to lowering the curtain. Some people keep that curtain drawn over themselves to hide the dark side of themselves, and some people keep it drawn, so that they can shade against the hurt brought on by others.

The politics in her family had shown Shirley that though others may be trying for harmony; they often brought with them their own agendas. So with the acceptance of her standing at Lakehead, she was able to go back to her home town of London, and attend U.W.O. The contrast between the two couldn't have been sharper.

All the turmoil of emotions, change, and loss of fear of the unknown, had made Shirley different than she had been before. After much pep talks from her dorm sisters, she would in the future, begin to assert her own needs. Being assertive had been one of the most unnatural things that she could grapple with. It felt wrong to her that she would have to push so hard, with some people, in order to be heard.

She used to think, how difficult could it be for a person to have consideration of the equality for another person? There were so many people who could not make peace with themselves; therefore, they would make damn sure that other people were unsettled. She would literally cry for hours on end when others would commit an offense against her.

After her right of passage in university far away from home, she was able to emerge like a butterfly. It was with grace that she left the halls of that institution of higher learning, and take a giant step back to her cyclical life back home. She felt as though internally she had changed gears, and no one in her home town had moved an inch. She was like an alien from another galaxy for that year back in London, Ontario. Her friends had written her off as a non-entity. They had all but completely abandoned her. The one true friend that she did hold on to had made her feel as though she were at fault for her own issues.

The transformations of those early 20s came at her at the speed-of- light. There was no time to discuss, or analyze. Shirley had decided that she would make another bold move in one more school year's time. There were no great loves there, just dates. The Country Club U had come to live up to its reputation of having more wealthy kids in attendance than any other school. A night out with the son of a large clothing manufacturer, was like something out of a movie script, when he picked her up in his Porsche. She really felt out of place there; not for the first time in her life, but she made the most of her time.

She dug into books about the formation of Canada, and the long winded lectures of her history professor, who would stand in front of them for three hours, from 6 p.m. to 9 p.m. at night. The laws that were written from the time leading up to confederation, were studied with a fine tooth comb. It was overwhelming how much legislation had to be in place to form Canada. The Geology professor would rave on about how the earth is going to be uninhabitable, so as students were being proactive about building a habitable planet. Professor Melville of the Geology department of U.W.O. gave mother earth, 25 more glorious years before its destruction.

She used to walk along the same sidewalk with him, just in front of her, for most of the way. This was a man who wore sensible shoes, and did not own a car. His lessons made a huge impact. During her studies, Shirley was most herself in any literature class. The hippie professor who taught her poetry, was complimentary about her abilities to get to the heart of any critique. Her love of thick books written by authors of the most complicated classics, helped define the woman that she was rapidly becoming.

Anna Karenina kept her enraptured for months. Leo Tolstoy had a special place in Shirley's mind. She savored the richness of his volumes, and used his words to provide her with strength. There was a smooth didactic flow to his work, that would soothe any ache she had had. If a person puts themselves in a state of concentration, then they stimulate the part of the brain that makes the cerebral cortex robust. She drank in the intellectual lessons.

Theory seemed much easier to understand than reality. Instances that would baffle her would come up every day; the more exposed she became to the work world. Some people lived in a vacuum of self loathing that they would not care to consider what impression they give unto others. She had tried to hold on to her values, and in a number of circumstances, she would be questioned as to why she was non-tolerant to such ignorant behaviour.

The stories of Tecumseh, and of Canadian heroes who had fought through tough circumstances, lit a light in her soul. These images were even easier to bear than the realities facing her in daily discourse. Terrorism had lingered as a true picture as the world was rapidly enveloped by technology.

The 1980s were bland, and tough, as the world was bombarded by the fear of nuclear genocide. It was not even comprehensive to Shirley as a young girl how this bleak existence could be habitable. She knew in her heart that as the threat of human annihilation kept on playing over and over in music videos, magazines, and in Hollywood films; that the concept took on a mere cartoon-like quality as the decade drew to a close.

Even this teenage mind could grasp that Ronald Reagan as a

figure head, a supposed mastermind, could not pull off such a threat. Yet, through all of her reasoning, there did exist real people south of the border who lived as though they had to constantly look over their shoulder.

Growing up with nuclear capabilities at the forefront of all terror threats, with greed as the creed of the day, was certainly in stark contrast to the world in which she was born. She sprang into the world in the early autumn of 1967, a blessed year when crowds of concerned, docile, doped up youths, came together to talk about love.

In her own youth, at the pinnacle of her memory of music, John Lennon's untimely, violent death sent shock waves through her 13 year old soul. Her closest friend was the daughter of two concert pianists, and together they relived every millisecond of Beatlemania. The messages of peace, love, the simplicity of human relationships, along with the complexity of human relationships, made an everlasting impression on young Shirley.

Throughout her life, she would turn to the Beatles for the comfort of their wisdom, their brave stands against tyranny, and their knowledge of the language of love. This was an enduring legacy, and more than just songs, she treasured their art.

Now by the late 1990s, Shirley was ready to move into the new millennium with new hope, and now, with a whole new set of values that she had garnered from living in South America. It seemed such a strange mix. The war of words amongst humankind had become sharper now that media outlets were broadcasting at an increasing rate.

The South American perspective was now firmly ingrained into her complex being. Bert had sealed the deal with her when shortly after Sabina left Buenos Aires; he ran into her bed in the middle of the night.

Shirley had not been prepared for the depth of physicality that she would experience with this fine German gentleman. The brief love that she had made with him, could not compare to her experience of any Canadian man. Not even close to what she experienced with Bert. Their love making was to her like the answer to the big question, that she had not had an answer to, up until this point in her existence.

It was a pure expression of love that defied reasoning. Time, and again as she matured even a decade into the future, she would remember the love she had felt in the moment. It was to be only but a blip on the radar; so sweet yet so short, but her keen awareness of being would always welcome a visit to it. She had loved Bert with a burning desire. Bert loved her with a pureness he would never experience again in his lifetime. Both lovers knew through what had happened between them; no other people were privy to what they knew.

A case in point that sometimes love has to stay undercover. She had no logical response to the rejection she felt from Bert, when they both knew that their short affair was over. She was desolate.

Not only did she feel that she had lost a confidant, but she had also lost the most prolific lover she had ever had the privilege of engaging with. Although it was no small comfort, Shirley also knew that somehow Bert had felt some sort of pain.

It was, August 30, 1997, and Shirley was out on the town with her new acquaintances from the elementary school named Northlands; where she was a teaching assistant to grade ones, and grade fives. There she was with two lovely British girls who she went to a club with in the posh neighbourhood of La Recoleta; they had broken the dawn at an all night dance club, when news of the car accident that killed Princess Diana, was broadcast to them all the way there in South America.

The immediate reaction to this devastation was that it clearly was a freakish accident. Something innate in Shirley had dictated that Diana did not die by accident. Her life resounded with depth. There had to be a moral higher purpose for her death. Diana's funeral occurred at 5 a.m. Buenos Aires time on September 6, 1997 that same day the beloved Mother Teresa also perished. The funeral bore upon her bearing deeply felt, and with the entire world outpouring their affection; there they all were in oneness watching her as if they knew her personally, and sobbing. Shirley, and her Aunt Patsy watched the entire ceremony through many tears, so much so, that they felt purified afterward; as the brandy worked its effect.

Six: BREAKING NEW GROUND

Words of Valor: Violence is the root of all evil.
The commotion of revelation is felt in the ground.
Actions in accordance with the mind, drive us far.

New experiences were to abound for Shirley in the land so far away, which was brought on, out of the clear blue sky, when Leo announced that he would be making the trip to Argentina. He had only returned to Vancouver a short six months before. This was to be a mission of sorts. This trip would seal the deal so that Shirley would finally be able to make the move back to Vancouver, after a long exploration of Argentina. It was clear, that by the passage of two years time, Shirley had indeed, over stayed her welcome in the country.

The end of Shirley's time in Argentina was marked by significance. Leo came, and was greeted with open hospitality as Shirley, and Patsy and, their family showed him the local sights of Buenos Aires. Leo came there fully loaded with ideas about the city. He always made it a clear priority to study something about the local history, and art, of any place that he visited.

When he landed in Argentina, he made sure to quiz her about all that they would see together. Leo specifically cherished the adoration that the people of Argentina had felt toward Evita. He enjoyed the skewed Hollywood view of this fallen saint. The way that she flaunted her diamonds, and came from a poor family, only to end up as the wife of one of the most notorious dictators in

Argentine history.

Peron's tactics were sleazy, yet he wore a great grin, and he used his beautiful young bride's charisma to his advantage. While he, Juan Peron was in the back rooms of smoking parlours, and brothels, making the deals. The whole world was fearful of Peron; his country was on top, selling its' proverbial soul.

Shirley was by this time in her intellectual development, rife with point of view. It was after all, a point of view, that had a front row seat to the action. Coincidentally, in 1996, pop star Madonna was shooting the movie Evita right in downtown Buenos Aires. Upon arrival, from the long arduous drive from the airport, she remembered reading the spray painted dialogue on every highway overpass asking for Madonna to leave; exclaiming that she was not a saint, and so for that matter, neither was Evita. Evita was everywhere, and no where, in her fellow citizen's hearts, as she had been perceived to be.

Divine glorification was not evident in the cemetery which bears her remains. The downtown neighbourhood of, La Recoleta, holds one of the most sacred of cemeteries in all of South America. It was to be a true sign of honour to have relatives that were buried there, and many Argentines had only one dying wish; to lie within its' beautiful sandstone walls for eternity.

La Recoleta is where Evita was interned, but her grave is not marked with splendor, and is in fact, by all appearances, quite obscure considering all the hype of her funeral. It was also well publicized that her body to this day, remains in pristine shape almost as she was in life; due to the amount of chemicals within it. Apparently, the story goes, that someone opens her coffin and actually brushes her hair, but then during the height of World War II, and Nazi Germany; the body had to be shipped out of the country for fear it would be destroyed.

It was as if even in death, that anyone associated with Juan Domingo Peron, would surely be a target. It was well known that he was indeed a Nazi sympathizer. As a matter of fact, many Nazi's were carefully removed from Germany after World War II, to enjoy a peaceful existence in Argentina. Shirley had met some German Argentines in her own gated community. By well over four decades, they were more Argentine in aspect, and manner yet, appeared to be German in physical features.

Upon making conversation at a cocktail party, she remembered some proud Argentine intellectuals expressing their disdain, for their own version of the Virgin Mary. Evita had captured the hearts of the downtrodden, poverty stricken people, who didn't have the capacity to partake in organized education. She had spear headed many low income housing projects right back as far as the late 1940s. For Leo, the mystic bubble surrounding his beloved fascinating Evita had faded by his encounters, but still he did not have the political insight that Shirley had by then.

There were other regions of South America that Leo had made it a point to venture to with Shirley. The two found themselves at a local travel agency, not long after his arrival, to see all of the surrounding countries they could get to, within a three week stretch.

With advice from fellow teachers at her school; Shirley was drawn to the idea of Bolivia, and Peru. Now these were not resort-like destinations by any means, but they were certainly a once in a lifetime chance to see trek adventure-type destinations. After all, it wasn't as if you could stop by a Starbuck's, on Machu Pechu, or anything.

Shirley found herself in an empowering position with Leo in Argentina. It wasn't a strange new world to her, and she was used to the bold expressions, and loud volume of the people. Leo found himself out of sorts in the company of such passion, as he was so accustomed to the British, and West Coast laid-back, understated manners. Some Argentine people could come across as brazen to those who were not immediately perceptive. Before at times it would serve as an annoyance to Shirley, as she would be frustrated by the way she would be treated; as though she was an imposition.

It was evident now, almost two years later, that she had been less quick to be judgmental, as she understood some of the trials, and tribulations of the realities of South America. This was an entire continent that should be able to boast about its' rich resources, and vastly, intricately woven culture. This was not the case here, as the native populations were still looked down upon, and were actually called a name because of the colour of their skin.

This was a land that had not learned to embrace a diverse mix of races, but rather shunned diversity.

The long admired native songstress of Argentina: Mercedes Sosa, had sung about her hopes for a peaceful future. "Todo Cambiar," was an anthem to the dark skinned Argentines, who looked forward to the day of redemption, when they could smile upon their heritage. Her soulful voice rang loud, and clear; the tribal rhythm soothed Shirley's inner mind. There was much that had changed in her mind, and her heart had expanded. It seemed such a shame that she had to bear witness to suffering on a large scale, to have gained this wisdom.

Leo had lovingly remarked about the tone in his close friend's voice, and how she had begun to speak like someone in the know. It was just like Shirley's first impression of the Argentine women, and how they commanded attention, especially from the men that they loved. It was with sweet remembrance that she had seen each person kiss each other lightly on each cheek, every time they encountered someone they knew well. What a lovely gesture to bestow upon another person; as polite a sign of affection, as there could be.

It was with mounting excitement then, that she, and Leo packed their suitcases on their five day tour of Bolivia, and Peru. The flight was booked right from the downtown Buenos Aires airport, which ran from a strip in the middle of two sides of the main freeway. It wasn't like just any highway that Shirley, nor

Leo, had ever navigated before.

Buenos Aires has the widest Avenue in the world with 16 lanes wide at its deepest. It was a super traffic bonanza, in the midst of French Colonial architecture. The colossal imposing Oblisque stands strong, along with the most beautiful Argentine flag, holding the spotlight it deserves, as well. The airport to La Paz, Bolivia, was not far at all from the action. The plane felt as though it were well above 35, 000 feet as usual flights soar to, and there were no long safety demonstrations, nor were any of the overhead stowage units inspected. Leo felt as though he, and Shirley would perish. She had not been witness to her dear friend's petrified reaction to flying before, or had she known, he had a fear of heights.

La Paz, Bolivia, is the city which lies at the highest altitude of any city in the world. To provide vivid perspective, La Paz, is 10 km above sea level. Shirley had quietly mentioned to Leo that fifty percent of the people who visit the city become very sick with vertigo, from the environment.

It was true that the landscape from the airport did look like some craters on the moon, so dry and well above the tree line. The roads were rudimentary at best, the airport was very small, yet clean, and the hotel was not aesthetically pleasing either. In fact, to her the hotel reminded her of one of those cement Soviet block apartments.

She was eager to explore though, and she knew that she could not pass up the opportunity to see Lake Titicaca; that she had been told so much about from her coworkers.

Leo was not to make it outside their hotel, however, due to the fact that the altitude sickness had gripped him from the moment they stepped off the plane. It was safe to estimate, that he was not enchanted. His skin turned to a pale pallor, and he wanted nothing more than to lie in a dark room on the bed.

But Shirley had jovial thoughts on her mind, and after tending to her sickly friend more than once since their arrival in Bolivia, she decided to hire a tour guide. There was no shortage of drama in Bolivia, the first incident with Leo, was that he left his Canadian Passport on the A.T.M. machine in the airport before the pair got into a taxi to the hotel. Upon arrival at the hotel, Leo realized that the passport was missing. With immediate, yet concise action, Shirley asked the taxi driver to take them back to the airport. She was good in crisis mode, and putting out the fires so to speak.

When Leo, and Shirley got back to the airport, they were able to retrieve Leo's passport without incident. There were honest, good, helpful people in Bolivia, despite the desperate disheveled state it seemed to be in. It was right from the onset that Shirley was impressed by this country. With her fun spirit at the helm of this tour, she was able to hire a teenaged Bolivian boy to be her guide on the pot holed filled, rugged, muddy road, to Lake Titicaca.

The ride to the shores of the highest lake in the world, was what

Shirley had imagined it might have been, on an off road expedition, to some isolated, rustic part of the world, such as India.

After all, Bolivia was a poverty stricken country that had long lamented being landlocked by the countries of its borders. The dispute over allowing just a strip of land on to the ocean was never so close, and never, so far away.

Bolivians felt as though they were perpetual victims in the eyes of the world, but only on the political stage, was this evident. On this road trip the Bolivian people jumped on, and off the uncovered jeep without announcement, just as if they had taken this unimaginably dirty road as their daily commute. Some along on that particular day, were loaded down with everything they owned, packed upon their sides, and upon their backs. She could see that these were stout, dark, and hardy people.

They had a peaceful demeanor inherent to their manner. None of these people stared at this young white Canadian adult woman, who looked so out of place. Remarkably she did not feel alone amongst them; in some quiet way, they had made her feel quite at home.

Once the jeep had traveled about an hour outside the city, she could see the shores of the enormous lake, which was populated all along in a rural pattern by humble small homes, and docks. A little way further, though it did seem like such a frozen moment in time for Shirley, they had reached their destination; where it was prearranged that her, and her young guide, who was dressed in a formal school uniform, would stop for lunch.

This was not a restaurant that they had stopped at, it was a family home with a screened-in porch, that had a table laid out neatly with linen napkins. From this screened in observation point, she was witness to a sight that took her at least twenty minutes to discern exactly what was going on. There were four people standing upright on a wooden boat just larger, and deeper than a Canadian canoe, pulling up, and down, gently on fishing wire.

Shirley had never seen professional fishermen at work before. After approximately twenty five minutes of this, the Bolivian family disappeared. Ten minutes later, she and her guide were served by the woman on the boat, the finest pink trout she had ever tasted in her life. The dichotomy of the scene was ridiculous; here she was this young curious Canadian woman on a personalized tour, who just witnessed an entire family catching her fresh lunch, for which she only had to pay the equivalent of four Canadian dollars for.

It was a moment in her life that she had been completely, pleasantly, surprised by, just as if a fine gift had suddenly been laid at her feet. It was a privilege to be a Canadian; after all, this was a girl who had been brought up in government housing on Boullee Street in London, Ontario, Canada. There wasn't a degree of gratitude that Shirley was not cognizant of in that moment.

This was a realization that held great significance to the core of her being her most authentic self. This shining moment of self awareness did not happen in subtle waves, it is like a dramatic light that beamed through from a thicket of trees that turned her consciousness into a higher step up that ladder of oneness, and freedom.

This was something that could not be practiced, it was something that had to be acquired. She needed the Bolivian perspective as an epiphany to bolster the connectedness to all that she had, with awed fascination, only read about before. Her young Bolivian guide made stifled conversation in Spanish, as they sat eating their meal together, about the devastation brought on by the drug cartels, and how complete villages were decimated, simply for the supply of coca leaves. His view was that he felt it was unfair that though he was able to attend university in his own country, the thought of a future was hopeless.

Shirley knew that obstacles, when thought of in a certain way, were insurmountable, but only to those not brave enough, to put themselves at risk. Without a second thought, there were many situations for which she had, herself, put all she had in the world at risk, and truly didn't know it. The process of thinking it through, before taking the giant leap, was the killer.

She had hoped that in retrospect, this young Bolivian man would remember that she had expressed from within her self, that hope is only a last resort, and that proactive risk-taking was the way to drive forward into one's future. She had wanted to evolve to be the type of person who could only give advice when it was solicited, to be there when needed, and to be ready for anything.

There existed no outside entity that she could put a label, or a name on, that would satisfy her being in this world. She knew right at that moment, upon the shores of Lake Titicaca, that she would have to earn her keep to stay above the fragility of human weaknesses.

Whereas, up onto this precipice in her development, she had so wanted to rely on outside influences: material things, status quo, career advancements, and romantic love, to define who she was; all of these outside things had failed her. The hollowness of her righteous soul had to be shed. It was time to emerge from the wreckage. The time was ripe to stop shedding the tears, to blame all of those who had come before her, and to enter into the next phase.

The blame game was so easy, but it just served to move her backwards, so with perseverance, she would take this one shining experience, and make good practical use of it. She was to turn 30 soon, and while it may sound cliché, it needs to be expressed anyway; it was time to grow up emotionally, stop wearing that shroud, and start embracing the spirit, and champion, of all things fun.

Cuzco, Peru, was the next stop on the 1997, South American tour, and touch down there was much smoother, especially for her travel companion Leo. Machu Picchu garnered interest from intellectuals from across the globe, who were drawn to the basin of the Amazon River, not only for the natural wonder of the Andes, and the life giving supernatural wonders of the river, but for the man made wonder; that had only been presumed to be there, as a place where all the great philosophical minds of the Inca tribes, could be hidden away from the tyranny of the Spanish Conquistadors.

Cuzco, felt as though it was but a small outpost, but really it served as a link for tourists all over the world, who came to view this UNESCO Heritage site. It was an important, confusing, rustic, town with dirty streets, and a rundown, old cathedral as the prime focus, in the main square that was over run by pigeons.

Shirley was sensitive to these ancient battle worn streets, and could feel the ghosts of the past that had fought for their lives to gain independence, and who had settled there long before any inhabitants of the entire South American continent.

The world must have been small thousands of years ago. The remnants of walls that the Incas had built, remained as conspicuous evidence that they had been there. Now their handy work lingered in the minds of the modern tourist, but continuously dazzled the modern scientist. The rocks were cut with the preciseness, that could only be marveled at, but which remained mysterious as to how, exactly it got there.

Shirley, and Leo were amused by the tiny ancestors of the Inca tribes, as they stood amongst the ruins of the walls in full traditional costumes, posing for money. This carefully executed photo opportunity, was Leo's forte, as he grabbed onto the cutest baby llama, and flashed his bright, beautiful set of white teeth. There were few people in the world that had such a dazzling smile as her friend Leo.

She was presently never too shy to let the people she loved so much on compulsion to know what she thought were their best qualities. Feelings of appreciation could not be overly expressed if sincere. One of the most positive qualities about relationships was how humans could interact with one another, in a way, that could make each other feel highly valued.

In this spontaneous, pleasant vibe she wanted others to know their best qualities, and she was clearly unabashed about it. Her brother had once told her, "Shirley you make everyone feel good." That was something that she would play over in her head, and made reference to, whenever she needed the strength to carry herself through loneliness.

From Cuzco, the two of them boarded the train ride of a lifetime. It was a very old, very slow, crowded, and decrepit train. The distance was only supposedly about 80 kms, but it took well over two hours, and one frantic stop later, to get there. The famous train to Machu Picchu, had to stop, because there was fuel gushing out the sides of it, and small children from nearby villages were standing beside it, filling their buckets with toxic fuel it was certainly an eye opening scene.

It seemed to Shirley that this could only happen in a

superfluous, dream, but it really was happening. Leo became agitated, and was bracing himself for disappointment, as they arrived at the tiny village, at the base of Machu Picchu. She on the other hand, was not so agitated, but was actually quite amused, at what had taken place on the train.

One of the middle aged American tourists stood out to them on this cramped ride where there were barely enough seats, and in fact, the hard metal seats, faced each other. This tourist had the most hideous, giant, festering, scabs covering not only her lips, but much of her face, as well. As Leo and Shirley faced this strange lady, who otherwise well dressed, Leo burst out in not so hushed a tone, "What the hell happened to your face?", as the lady walked off the train. Shirley could only laugh her deep, belly laugh that she had worn on her sleeve, day in and day out, because it truly was a shocking sight, and the two of them had to contain themselves for hours. She remembered as a little girl during a solemn mass, having to contain her laughter to the point of tears, at such a time as was inappropriate. This instance felt like one of those times.

Upon arrival at Aguas Calientes, at the base of Machu Picchu, the travel weary duo found themselves in a dirty village, a mere five blocks long, so immediately, the pair found humble accommodations. This was followed quickly by a meal. It had certainly been an arduous day. The table at the inn was almost up to their chins, it seemed odd, but it was quiet practical to have one's food in such close proximity to one's mouth. Their appetites weren't huge after having to walk in excrement stained alleyways amongst loose chickens, and one very large, hairy, black pig. Leo joked remarked that the pig was running after her.

Shirley wanted to do what she did well, and that was to sit on a patio, and have a beer. Any place that she had ever traveled no matter where, always there had a place to sit outside, and have a beer. Leo had to haggle with her to get her into the purpose at hand, which was to climb up through the Inca trail to the mystic city above.

Though she appeared as though she were a stranger to the hikers creeds, there in the deep, lush, Amazon forest, her and her friend, expertly traversed the steady incline along the road, to the fantastic sight. Leo fancied himself to be the consummate outdoors man, and against Shirley's best judgment, decided to try to go off the beaten path on the way up. She had an uneasy feeling that going through this never before traveled bush, would not be safe. Leo pushed, until he finally battled her into the path not taken.

Shirley was some six feet behind, when through a barb wired fence, half the distance up the mountain side, she saw three heavily armed military men, just waiting to catch stupid people wandering off the Inca path, to do only what Shirley could not imagine what.

Very skillfully, and with calm, reservation she expressed the obvious that they should turn around, and go back to the well worn path. What had happened to her personally in Bolivia, had provided her with great integral strength, that she instinctively knew she would use over, and over again, should any situation like this arise. South America, was not safe, therefore, going into the bush there in Peru, wasn't like going into the bush in British Colombia.

This safety issue had not jaded Shirley, it had just made her aware. She had been subjected to a taxi scam when out one night with three of her British cohorts in Buenos Aires. The unsuspecting girls had been on their way to the big city, from a distant small town, where their mutual friend taught; they were speaking in excited tones, when the driver veered off into a corn field, in the middle of nowhere, claiming that he had a flat tire. Shirley had read about such scenarios, and was on high alert. She spoke the best Spanish she could, she proclaimed that she knew what the scam was, and that basically, the jig was up. After uttering her stance, her and her friends, proceeded to exit the taxi, and walk along the dirt road to nowhere. The taxi driver, then drove along beside them, knowing full well that he had to surrender, that these were not prime victims.

In Buenos Aires, she had been astounded by the amount of armed men walking about the streets. Never, in her life, had she seen up close, and for real, a large machine gun. The streets of Buenos Aires, contained guard houses sporadically located along the most of the streets, whereby, armed patrols would survey, on any given day. This was the South American reality. Being someone heavily influenced by her environment, it was difficult for Shirley to grasp these sights nonchalantly. So here in the jungle, along the mountain path to one of the official wonders of the world, she was faced by this reality, in this particularly rare context, that had given her shivers down her spine. Her instinctual awareness was piqued. After some deep breaths, she, and Leo went further on their way, and then, there they were, in what can only be described as paradise on earth.

Machu Picchu, was certainly holy ground; one could feel this magical essence straight away. The vistas contained a relentless beauty. The sun could not help but to shine upon its cliffs, and mountains, in an unprecedented way. Even with Shirley's keen sense from having traveled across such a bountiful country as Canada, had she never witnessed such a pristine, other-worldly, scene.

Was this for real, that from what ever angle one could turn, there would appear another sight of the wondrous, splendour of nature? Was this even possible? The scene was so difficult to put into words. The views were of epic, panoramic proportions, and what was doubly inspiring, was that the clouds, and the sun, worked in unison to create spectacular effects.

The IMAX film makers must have spent some time there, in order to have the inspirations, to develop their technology. Both were avid Star Wars fans, and amongst their favourite science fiction films was, Close Encounters of the Third Kind, which they had discussed as a point of reference to Machu Picchu, but definitely not one single, imaginary thought, or popular movie, could possibly express what their eyes witnessed here, in Peru, at the Basin of the Amazon River.

This was the reason why art tries to reflect reality. Shirley had felt a deep affinity for art that reflected beauty, but winced at depictions of anger. The pair laughed, and posed for photos, and stared into the sometimes hazy, sometimes sunny, abyss up above the earth. Leo chimed, "They should build an amusement park up here!" Shirley joked, "Where's the Tim Horton's?" They decided that one visit to this place, would certainly not be enough, and when after the first day, they had toured all of the ruins of the village, and had read all of the plaques, they decided that it would be on the agenda to come up there one more time.

This is what Leo had meant to do when he came to Buenos Aires, and it gave him a great feeling of accomplishment that the two had made it. He often felt hurried about his life, and was meticulous about quantifying people, and how he spent his days, in regard to his interactions with them. Shirley was worn down by the lists that he made. Life to her wasn't about sitting down, and writing down things to do.

Never had she understood the concept of a "To Do" list; wasn't that for someone who didn't actually do anything? That was her rationale. This need to fulfill a list, bothered her about her friend, though she was so busy actually doing things, to address this issue. Then she thought a "To Do" list is for someone who must really be insecure about their memories. These people must worry about their short term memory. That was an alarming thought. This was how her mind processed things being a Libra born on October 2nd, she was sure that had something to do with how she processed life. Librans were known to see every possible side, of every situation. It was brain chatter, and it could be exasperating. She imagined that if it bothered her, it must bother others, as well. She pondered, wasn't it true though, that when one truly loves another, that personal foibles are easily dismissed?

One night in Aguas Calientes, makes the hard woman humble. No, that was a line from the song "One Night in Bangkok," not to be confused of course. The village was located on a natural source of hot springs, so they engaged in going to the public pool very close by. Leo didn't particularly enjoy the run-down facilities, so after a short time in and out, they went back to their lodgings. The two retired in their chambers clearly wiped out. They had strategically decided to take the bus back down to the village, and truly both were glad that they had endeavored to walk the way up.

After many travel adventures, the two had become hardened by the circus, and corralling involved in tourism. However, this is the plight of tourists. Shirley had actually lived abroad here by this time, and wasn't just a visitor. She felt that her tastes were broadened through being an ex-pat. The extent of the exposure to the true nature of the culture, be it any culture, becomes significantly degraded when one puts themselves in the realm of a tourist. It was clear to her that the locals definitely put on their best false faces for the tourist, which translates into a false impression.

Shirley, and Leo aspired to have the best authentic experience here in Peru; she acknowledged that she had thus found herself with the best possible travel partner she could hope for, however, she now was at an advantage, because she had lived there in South America for almost two years, and knew what to expect. The constant bombardment of culture was not such a surprise by now. For her travel companion, day two was on the agenda, because he needed to fulfill his list, but for Shirley, it was a chance for her to just think about this entanglement she was in.

Day two at Machu Picchu, was just as singular an experience as day one, yet even more so, as the pair climbed away from the village, and from their brochure, read about the seven day Inca Trail trek. The day was marked by a helicopter taking off from the mountain, and when Shirley, and Leo spoke to onlookers, they heard that Princess Anne had been, and went. Princess Anne was the most underrated of all the British Royal Family, having tirelessly championed innumerable, charitable causes. They had only slightly missed having their photo taken with her.

It wouldn't be long until the two made their way back to Cuzco, where they decided to have a formal dinner before returning to

Buenos Aires, through their Bolivian, connecting flight. Having overcome his reluctance, Leo was in high spirits at the Peruvian restaurant, and much to Shirley's dismay, ordered Guinea Pig, the local delicacy. She took photos of him grinning, lifting his plate to display the creature, before commenting on every single bite. She couldn't give it a thought, that he was actually eating a rodent, and tried to look away for the duration of the meal.

It was these kinds of exchanges between the two that made her feel the bond that they shared, ever more. They were able to throw barbs in the air, and appreciate their differences. Leo was all too aware of this so he worked very hard to give his attention to other people, just to make her jealous. It was as though he were putting out his feelers, to test his affect on her. Shirley felt hopeless in these situations, but she wasn't about to give in to her friend, she definitely wanted to stand her ground. It was not her intention to have a relationship that was played out like a game of chess. Didn't everyone want equality? One would certainly think so. Healthy friendships should not have to be carried out with childish power struggles.

That final day of the Peruvian/Bolivian tour was over, and Leo, and Shirley boarded the Air Boliviano, flight back through Cuzco, to La Paz. In La Paz, they were met by a not so pleasant, surprise when the ticket agent told them that their flight had been canceled. It wasn't that they were offered any explanation as to why, and they were only told so after their luggage had been checked.

Shirley went on full Argentine woman alert, as she badgered the ticket agent with great force of will. She had been the sole participant in a full out public melt down. She screamed with ferocity, that the she and her friend, were not going to stay over night in La Paz, but instead, would get back to Buenos Aires, or else.

Leo had never witnessed any public outburst from her before, and she herself had never remembered being so riled up before. She could hardly believe the tone of her own voice. She was like a mama bear on the attack. The ticket agent had no other choice than to book this lunatic woman on the next Airlineas Argentina flight, and fast. In the blink of an eye, the two were boarding the next flight.

Leo was rattled not only by the will of his friend, but by the turbulence of the flight. As soon as they sat down, Shirley ordered champagne, in fact, she ordered an entire bottle. The flight attendant didn't hesitate to hoist the bottle right to their seats, and leave it there. This incident was something that only later on, the two of them reflected on, to laugh at. Leo was so frightened of that flight that he squeezed her hand with the tightest grip he could, and as Shirley looked into his face, she saw that his eyes were bulging out of their sockets. The dynamics of their relationship had changed significantly. She was no longer Leo's docile sidekick. She was a force to be reckoned with.

Seven: A SHINY NEW SLANT

Words of Valor: Gathering, and categorical organization, are the first steps.
Putting everything together is inevitable, instinctual.
Independence is the end of sufferance.

The day that Leo left Argentina, Shirley was sad, and relieved at the same time. She had changed who she was, but she also knew that soon, she would return to Vancouver to start her life anew, and that this man would still be an important element in her life. She wanted more independence, but there was no doubt that she would be with him, as much as she could. There wasn't much more for her to discover about Buenos Aires, and her ex-pat friends were dispersing back to their countries of origins.

She had turned 30 in the Patagonia, at Bariloche. As a special retreat, Aunt Patsy flew her there to a high end five star spa, resort. The views from the hotel patios were amazing, this was the Andean equivalent to the Rocky Mountains of Canada. Her and her aunt, observed birds of a breed that she had never seen before, they ate the finest food, and drank the finest wine. Shirley was entering the decade of her life, where adults would start to take her seriously, as being a full member of the adult club.

Aunt Patsy had been very generous to accommodate Shirley as her house mate, especially after witnessing the work involved in raising three children, she was not ready to be a mother, and now even in her 30s, she wasn't even sure that she ever wanted to be a mother. She knew it was time for her to go back to Canada. She was so isolated in Buenos Aires, and didn't feel that the concerns of Argentines came anywhere close to her own. She had by these two years time, explored, and experienced all there had been to experience, about South America for that span of time.

January 1998, was not a busy time to fly from Argentina to Canada, for obvious reasons. Buenos Aires was having balmy summertime weather, and in Canada, well it was the dead of winter. Coming through the boarder in Miami, she felt a tremendous amount of relief, and it must have shown on her face, as she remembered the boarder agent welcoming her there as, Miss Canada.

This was pre- 9/11 when crossing boarders was a breeze, and for the last of the lag of travel, when she arrived in Toronto's Pearson Airport, she remembered that she could hear the sound of silence. She had not been aware that she had been immersed in an amazingly high amount of noise pollution for two years. Silence sounded like people were whispering. From first glimpse, Toronto was so squeaky clean, and fresh. It was a privilege that Shirley could now have this point of view of her dear Canada, but through being miserable in her last moments in Argentina, she had put a lot of weighty expectations on her return.

She had no foresight to do the research about the phenomenon of culture shock. It would have been wise to know what she would be up against, as she returned to London first, and then on to Vancouver, but it somehow was not a priority. Survival, yet again, was number one on the agenda.

It had seemed that although she had seen people engaged in independence; she did not know any other way to get by in life, however, she was not keen on the whole idea of being alone. It would have seemed a foregone conclusion to anyone who had traveled to so many places, and who had no roots, so to speak, that independence was the inevitable.

It still did not register in her brain, that loneliness was nothing like independence. So again, during three weeks back in her home town, and discovering that she was so out of touch with her family's daily lives, she did nothing but sleep, and whimper. To her older siblings she was inconsolable and by all means a wreck. She acted like she was shipwrecked. Time is meant to be wasted sometimes, and this futile time period was just to set the stage for her to return to Vancouver, where she had always longed to be. Something about the ocean, the mountains, made it the most stunning, and healthy place to be.

So once again, there she was peering out the window down at the Rocky Mountain range, a scene that she had carved in her mind, and that she had lived to see more than a few times already. Upon arrival at the Vancouver Airport, she immediately discovered that her lifeline Leo was not as thrilled by her return, as she had hoped he would be. She was in a compromised position now without a place to stay, and the onus would be on her dear friend to put her up, until she could land on her feet.

This time around was not so easy for Shirley, after all, she was not a young, bleary eyed girl, with rainbow dreams, anymore. The seasons had changed fiercely, and the ideal set up in the coast city, was not as feasible as it had been in the early 90s.

Nevertheless, after a few months, she was placed in a whole new world, when Leo vouched for her to work at one of the oldest brokerage houses in Vancouver; right on the old Vancouver Stock Exchange, in the heart of the business district. This job placement was not by mere accident, but it truly felt accidental. Shirley was an artist at heart, and here she was, taking on the position as accounting clerk. There couldn't have been a more incongruous job on the planet for this a woman, who had laughed her way through math class in high school, and since, had never looked back.

In the midst of this staggering change, one in which Shirley took on with poise, and grace, she was suffering from the reverse of culture shock. There were days when she would walk through the crowded streets in downtown Vancouver, and wonder why she was there. The tears would just flow out like rain, in spontaneity. She wasn't sure now that she was back here, if she really belonged. She felt disembodied, and clearly uninvolved, for months. The only thing that could drag her out of her daily misery was red wine. After work she would finish off an entire bottle by herself, and fall into a deep stupor, of something that was supposed to resemble sleep. Alcohol had lost its glossy effect on her, that it once had. She was using red wine as an elixir. Being an accounting clerk is as dull a position as any person could ever do, but she knew that she had her friend's connections to consider, so she made her way to the office without fail.

Being eye-witness to the hawks of capitalism was somehow embarrassing. She had never known for sure, that they actually felt assured that there was no limit to the amount of money they could make. Didn't their mathematic minds calculate that sustainability was where the world was headed? Some of them truly felt that they were above the natural laws of physics, or at least ignored the cold hard facts of the matter.

Shirley could hear the Ronald Reagan speech in her head, belching out to the world from his pulpit, that Americans were on the top, and would stay on top, endlessly. These brokers were looking out amongst the ocean, and the mountains, but they weren't seeing how hollow their existence was. They were all terrible actors, who didn't even know their lines, in a freak show.

The bottoming out of Japanese markets in 1998, hadn't even discouraged these scavengers. She became the wall between the broker, and the investor, who had lost hundreds, and thousands of dollars, in the blink of an eye. The head of the research department shrugged off the Asian economic crash, and predicted it would only be a matter of months before recovery. He said that it was a matter of course. Shirley had the inside track, even though she was supposed to act as though she didn't know. Her inner turmoil ceased, for she knew that this was certainly not a situation, she felt she wanted to earnestly be in, the midst of, not as a willing participant. At such times, in circumstances such as these, it is best to not know, so she put up her protective armor, and carried on.

Work only became interesting for her, when she began to acquaint herself with some of the characters at the firm. The brokers came mostly from the upper crust of life, and really what they had to do was juggle people's money around like balls in the air, being optimistic that they wouldn't crash down. A lot of these so called "suits" spent most of their days looking busy, and acting concerned. It was a false world, that was for sure.

Fridays would be desolate there at the office tower, early on in the day, a frenzy shuffle out of the building would occur, and always, someone seemed to be on holidays. Many could brag about their fabulous lives, wives, and kids. Some were completely embroiled in the all night party scene, as was evident by the white, pasty faces that would stream through there, on many occasions.

Shirley had the keen awareness to separate the phoney ones, for the ones who had true merit. She would be treated miserably by the head accountant, who saw her as nothing, but the brunt of his disgust. These people were there, because they had no other place that they could be. She felt strangled with fear, when she could feel that some were talking about her, behind her back. It was as if she were in a tank full of sharks, some days. Nevertheless, she had toughened up considerably, and vowed that nothing would make her down on her life. It would have been so simple to loathe some of these coworkers, but wasn't she, in some weird way, supposed to envy their position in life?

The best that one can do in amongst these types of circumstances, is to stand tall, and stand above, the mess. At least in this context she did not feel as an outsider. She was proud to consider herself on the outside. So even after taking on a higher position within the same firm, and failing miserably with one particular broker; after one year she was on her way out the door, and never looked back. So much more was going on in her life, that this year could not be looked back upon with anger. She still had her dear friends by her side. Putting all repressed emotions aside, she flew into a crowd of characters, that moved at the speed of insanity.

Sharon had moved in with her boyfriend Dominic, who was a spoiled mama's boy, from North Vancouver. It wasn't as if he had much going for him, as far as Shirley could tell. Like the brokerage firm's rich kids that she saw day in, and day out; Dominic was from a well established family, who had made their fortunes early in the 1950s, in property development, along the North Shore. His life was spent showing properties, and basically showing off. Shirley felt like a target to his 'nouveau riche' lifestyle choices. Suddenly Sharon was well aware of designer everything, from her shoes, to her sunglasses. Her ostentatious, new-found character adjustment, was definitely unseemly.

She would attend dinners with Dominic, and his crew of friends, that he had hung around with since they attended private elementary schools with. Shirley was never one not to engage in brilliant conversations, but she seemed to just sit with all of these players, without a word to say. Often times, she would be watching the clock, or heaven forbid, start to yawn. On one such occasion, at the Vancouver Tennis Club, she found herself left behind with no ride, and empty pockets.

It wasn't out of character for Dominic's crowd, to treat people like they were disposable. It was excruciating to have to bear witness to what had become of her wonderfully brilliant friend. Shirley didn't want Dominic to know that he had been the cause of distress; no, that would only add fuel to the fire. She knew that Sharon would probably end up marrying Dominic, so in her usual Shirley-manner, she held true to her friendship, and suffered in silence.

It could have been that she played the same game as these powerful name droppers. The opportunity was certainly there, but she just couldn't find a way to manifest anything to add to the crowd mentality, and really found it boring to be in their company. She was a trooper after all, and never did she divulge how she felt to anyone in her social circle. It is best to keep integrity rather than to compromise it, all for the cause of vanity.

She had learned through the actions of her father, that she could look just as good as the big players in society. In talking to one of Dominic's friends on one evening, she just couldn't believe what she had heard. Penelope had thrust herself into this circle, and was proud of the fact that she didn't make friends with people, who didn't have something to offer her. Friends were not gifts, they were commodities. One thing that Shirley could say about her was, that she certainly was honest. It wasn't in her nature to judge people, but some people just beg to be pegged.

What was glaringly apparent about these society people was, that they walked around with a veneer around them, and none of them had really been exposed to culture. Shirley could easily identify with both sides of travel exposure. For example, it was so painful to have to see fellow tourists in Spain eating at Pizza Hut. She could imagine one in Dominic's faceless crowd of friends going to Argentina, and eating breakfast, lunch, and dinner at Denny's. It would be too easy to tease them, without them even being aware of this, but to be cruel, wouldn't satisfy anyone.

By a twist of fate, Teresa ended up working for one of the best computer game companies in Vancouver. After finishing her degree in Engineering, she was scooped up right away for her talents. Shirley felt blessed to be in her company, and was fascinated by all of her friends, the computer nerds. She would go into Teresa's office with doughnuts, or Starbuck's, since her dear friend had been tied down mercilessly to her projects. There were days when Teresa would literally sleep at the office. This was reasonable as competition was tough, and Vancouver was on the cusp of becoming a major centre for computer technologies.

Teresa felt under pressure a lot of the time, but didn't feel isolated. She was sure that all of her toiling would pay off in the long run. The world was becoming a much smaller place, and interactions with computers were a commonplace, daily activity. Shirley found that the people who were absorbed so much in their jobs, had to have an outlet for all of their pent up anxieties. Thus, hard working Teresa became the party specialist on her time off.

It seemed that she had an endless supply of money, and events to attend. These events, so to speak, were places where people could go, and find as much designer drugs as could be found in any one place, but there were other things that attracted Shirley to these happenings; namely, her artistic sensibilities. She had entered the Vancouver rave scene, and just in time for the year 2000, for it now was 1999, and she was firmly in the know.

Leo had his own band of rave soldiers, which he judiciously kept from his friend. He had felt a pull away from Shirley, as he had become more comfortable with his own sexuality. Because she had shown her vulnerable side to Leo, he wasn't thrilled with the prospect of having to be supportive of her.

The fair-weather friend syndrome had certainly taken hold of Leo, he was the one who had introduced Shirley to the world of privileged kids, within the brokerage industry. He felt no allegiance to her now, and like the adage that he had held on to, she had become a guest who had over stayed her welcome. During her re-emergence back to Vancouver, he had to pick her off the ground, on more than one occasion. He looked down upon her in disgust. For months on end, Shirley would not hear from him, but now she seemed like a good sidekick. once more, in the land of ravers.

Shirley once again had to be reacquainted with her friend Larry, the intrepid outdoors man, who was happily in the springtime of his relationship, with his darling woman, Yuki, whom he had met through acquaintances at the hotel. Yuki, was an import straight from Japan, which provided endless fascination for Thunder Bay, Larry. Yet for all the exotic background that Yuki had, she was equally enraptured with Larry's background, and his friends.

She managed to fit in perfectly with Shirley, Sharon, and Teresa. The four girls would go on shopping expeditions to keep their fingers on the pulse of fashion. There was a lot more technology being displayed in regard to body adornments; Vancouver had quickly become on the leading edge imminently because of the respect that was shown for the mish-mash of cultures, and as a nod to technological advances.

It truly displayed itself as one of the more thoroughly modern cities. The Native Canadians had cemented their place there with support from the government's programs, designed to showcase their art. The Asian population was exploding on to the scene, where once their cultural influences were concentrated in the Chinatown in East Hastings corridor, now there were sure signs in architecture, restaurants, and art displays all over the downtown core.

Where once the Vancouverites were protectionist, and resistant, they had come to have more understanding of people's attraction, to their city.

The homegrown Canadian girls were most attracted to Yuki's leading-edge eye for technology, which was directly a product of her Japanese ancestry. She held a perspective so utterly pure, when it came to the natural environment of the west coast; her mind was expanded by what she perceived to be, the large amount of space, of even the most densely populated area of the Westend. Shirley was content with the variety of the possibilities, that her small closely knit group of friends provided her.

In direct contrast, Leo was stifled by Shirley's need to rely on just a small amount of friends instead of racking up a huge social scene. He was becoming more about adding to his eternal lists of social events, and people, on his lifelong agenda. Although he wanted to be a separate entity from Shirley, his impulse was driven toward emotional, and mental control of her. He wanted to become more essential to her life, the more he saw her becoming more independent.

During the autumn of 1999, Leo grabbed on to Shirley's social life, as he made a big display of the rave scene that he had immersed himself in. It wasn't that he wanted to interfere in her other friendships, it was just that he really couldn't help himself.

She was not cognizant in any way, shape, or form, of this hidden agenda. She would not think about her own needs at all in regard to Leo. It was the type of relationship that she had always admired on her part, like taking the place of a family member, or even of a parental guide.

Her imagination was the only instinct that she relied on to manifest what it meant to be in a steady long lasting relationship. Ideally she wanted to be so driven toward pure love that was unconditional, even in a life time partner, and grasped at anything to fulfill this in her real life. On more than one occasion she had felt that as she grew up her older siblings had much more going on in their own nuclear families that she fit in less, and was considered as extended family.

It stung when at the age of nine, her nurturing sister Carol had told her she was getting married and was sad not to see her as often as she would like anymore. By now, extended family was indeed what she was, but it was less difficult for her to cope with this unintentional rejection there in B.C. blazing her own trail.

She believed that she achieved it all along within her circle of friends. They had recognized her need to trust, and be trusted from day one. For Shirley though, the ultimate challenge, along with sacrifice, was attractive for some unknown line of reasoning. Leo was aware of that aspect of dire need in her. He played into this like a proverbial expert.

He started by taking up all of her spare time at this particular point, and by drawing the division between her, and her friends. Shirley's close knit social circle knew that she had been acting like a zombie, where Leo was concerned. At first, many had spoken out against the hold he exhibited, but then they witnessed just how intelligent he was. He knowingly forced people into praising him. It was like a secret power he had. Like the scene in Star Wars where Obi Wan casts a spell on the guard using his Jedi force.

Whenever he met one of Shirley's friends, he would send out a magic vibe like a halo effect, that shone solely upon him. It was as though people were tricked by him, especially those who weren't so well acquainted with Shirley, in the first place. There was a special place in her heart that needed to be filled. Those who admired her had not been fully aware of this, heightened fear of rejection kept her on the sidelines, in matters of the heart.

She had not set out on her interactions in life to be admired. This was just a fact. The thought of admiration was something she had set aside for her friends, and her family. It was so typical anyway to want to be admired. People were equal and who really had time to stand back behind the scenes, and plot for this?

Shirley just wanted equality in her most important relationships. There was a gravity of communicative aspects that weren't necessarily fraught with forbearance. What one person would morally put themselves above others? It truly was inconceivable.

Every person had some gift to give. Growing up in her family home, there were some pieces of art that she remembered staring into, and pondering their meanings. One was, "Little Boy Blue" who personified dignity and eloquence. His eyes didn't have to search around in question. This boy was assured of his stance, and if he could speak, she was sure that he would have something comforting, or deeply profound to say. His suit was made of a shiny dark azure, with its buttons made especially to provide the outline of his heart. The boy wore the finest silk, and the way in which he stood, was a measure of his fine manners. This was the boy that she had imagined would grow up to be the man of her dreams.

The fine assured mannerisms were taken seriously into her being. As Shirley matured, she became less tolerant of vulgarity, though as a child there were personal habits that she abhorred. In all of the novels that she had collected, the style of English was as eloquent, and fine, as she had ever heard, this was what she aspired to. She wanted to learn all about finery.

Another of her family treasures was, "The Desiderata" which was hung in the living room in a place of prominence. These were words that she held on to. It may be looked back upon in the 1980s, as a trite treatise, so irrelevant to the capitalists. As a baby of the 1960s, she identified with communality, peace, and sharing with others. She would look back at her sister's wedding photos from 1973, where she wore a halo of daisies around her head like a crown.

The daisies were strong, innocent, feminine, and reflected happiness. They were the flowers of the 1960s. In contrast, more and more, sarcasm became an expression of bitterness, that replaced the brilliant hopes for the future.

Leo had introduced his friend to the capitalist way of living. His family owned several vacation homes, apartments, and condominiums. He used the lure of his wealth to rein her in, because he knew that she wasn't at all fazed by it. More and more, she was becoming repelled by it. On a ski trip to the family's Whistler home, she was subjected to the first signs of Leo's brutality. She had never been on Whistler mountain before, the only skiing she had experienced before was in London, at the ski club, on a hill the size of an ant colony. Whistler was massive, literally, in four hours one could finish a meager two runs. What had possessed her to partake in this trip, she would quickly regret.

The house was fully occupied by Leo's family, the men were the loudest, and the woman of the house, Leo's mother, was there to serve the crowd with her fabulous skill for cuisine. She made the most of the two day trip, but she could hear the thunderous voice of Leo's brother as he commented, that Shirley was good to have around because she was quiet. He had chastised her in public, on the mountain, she cried until he finally just left her on a black diamond run, to fend for herself. She soon found that there was no way that she would ski down that steep run, but instead she would take her skis off, and walk down, no matter how far. Things worked out, she literally bumped into a kind British man with the same skill set, just as stuck, and as scared as she was, and together they endured this harrowing situation.

All eyes were on Shirley at dinner time as Leo proclaimed what a failure of judgment he had made to invite her there. Leo's brother was honest, and as rotten as he could be, to comment on how she could certainly throw back the wine. She was so relieved to get back to Vancouver, out from under the glare of prying eyes. This wasn't the strata of life that she wanted to be placed in.

It made her sad that she had not had the strength of character to stand up for what she believed in to be right. Leo had made her feel that she wanted to apologize for who she was. Her true friends would have called him out on this unseemly behaviour from the start.

Even after such an experience, Shirley remained true to her friendship with Leo. The two of them swept the Whistler debacle under the rug. Somehow though, whenever ski season started, and ended Leo made a bitter point of announcing, quite deliberately to her, that he would not be available. She would kick at the air that she would be waiting to hear from him, or would wonder what he was doing. Such arrogance! This could not be normal. The agonizing over one person, whom you had so definitively given over your will to, wasn't even close to healthy existence. Astonished by these revelations she was still too faint of heart to be proactive.

The year 2000, was so swiftly upon her, that Shirley in her gray cloud had not even made solid plans for it, because somehow, she didn't know what she had to celebrate. As a child, the new the millennium represented glamour, and dazzling beauty. Something fantastic was yet to be. Our forefathers and societal messages had always depicted that the future would be better; everything would be faster.

The scientists had even gone commercial. She had often surmised where she would find herself in the year 2000, and explore what would life be like. Here she was, this intelligent, risk-taking woman, bound by some tragic force, to someone who wouldn't be close to what she needed as partner through life. She would often plead with outside forces to deliver her from this mess. Justifications were fleeting thoughts. How many women did she observe, were actually content with where they found their destiny? Why were there so many thoroughly modern single, city-dwelling women, settling for sub-par relationships with men?

She didn't want to face her dread at all. So, with paraphernalia so artfully in place, she decided to rave in the New Year for 2000, or Y2K, in the posh Yaletown neighbourhood, of Vancouver. She had become the mistress of the vibrant rave scene by this point in time. Cher, had just risen from the ashes with her anthem of love called, "Believe", clearly pushing the boundaries of time, with her long beautiful red wig. She wanted to hold on to all of the wonderful things about her life, and escape. She felt there was no point in worrying about being compared to others. She donned a beautiful long red wig just like Cher, placed her Elton John blue sunglasses on her face, covered her body in decadent sparkly cream, wore a sassy shiny lilac dress, and topped it all off with her faux Chinchilla fur coat; all systems were go, for a night like no other.

When Shirley was in rave mode, nothing else mattered to her; she floated around on the dance floor for hours, with delicate ease. The music was a part of her freedom, her life; the rhythms pounded to the base of her heart. There, she was part of a congregation of some people who were nameless, and some people whose names she didn't even need to know.

Dancing was like floating, especially from hundreds of feet in the air, looking out from floor to ceiling windows; there overlooking the ocean, far from the madding crowd. This night, this long epic night, full of music, and dancing, was poetry. All those years of researching, reflecting on what New Years 2000 would be like, especially when she was a teenager, could not have come close to this.

There, now nearly ten years into her becoming an adult, she was escaping, and reveling in what her destiny was shaped to be. She had never been victim enough to fall for Leo, and his tyranny. During the night, he would spot her, and grab her, trying to bring her into the folds of what he deemed was love. She participated more in universality, rather than as, they two, as beings, facing the world as one. Shirley realized it was this insatiable need for control, that had kept him at least, physically at her side.

There was a metaphorical wall now in her mind, and she ultimately knew that time would separate them. It wasn't a movie that she was living in where circumstances sort themselves out only an hour later. It just wasn't as simple as a mere reflection of life; she was living this here, and now. There was an allowance for people's strange behaviours. Life wasn't painted in black, and white. No matter the anguish, the morality of right, and wrong, this relationship though confusing to her, would eventually become good for her.

Eight: EDITING MISTAKES

Words of Valor: There are times when letting it gush-out, is fine.
Tune into the refinement of the soul.
Don't give in to the pressures that force us to
define ourselves.

Mistakes made by a 32 year old woman, are no longer stupid ones. Mistakes were inevitable at any age, but by her third decade on this planet, Shirley had begun to make some really good ones. She kept following along with Leo, but was increasingly reticent in his company.

There were so many pursuits that she had independently reached out to enjoy in her Westend community. She joined the gym right around the corner from her apartment. At least twice per week, she would attend hour and a half yoga sessions with one of the most inspiring instructors. Kathleen, was principally a professional modern dancer, who integrated yoga practice along with reading from the teachings of Buddhism. The class was a refuge for her, to soothe her mind, and body. Her limbs were growing longer, her breathing was making a monumental difference to her overall attitude. This was all of her concentration as she teetered on the brink of loneliness.

The fragility of her principal relationship with a man, who couldn't give her what she needed. It was a difficult lesson to learn, but qualifying the needs of others above oneself, was a recipe for disaster. This was her error, she owned it, but that didn't mean she enjoyed it.

She was finding herself in a torrid affair with a man who was living with a woman. This had never been in her character before. Shirley knew full well that Simon had a live-in girlfriend, whom she had met in passing at a few parties. She didn't want to be hard on herself, but it wasn't going anywhere, all she wanted to do was to enjoy it while it lasted. She had resolved to do that for morality sake, so she was just going through the motions. However, the pull from Simon's end was so strong, that she found herself flattered by his valiant efforts.

He took her out to one of the most intimate, exclusive, boutique-style hotels, in the Westend, where they ordered the most expensive dinner, and wine. She found herself fascinated not only by the wooing, but by the strength of this man's conviction, and by the gravity of his situation at home; it was similar to a soap opera. He was deeply entrenched in a relationship, that was by his account, pulling him down like a drowning victim.

Shirley really didn't believe his story, but she did not mind one minute, that he claimed that one afternoon with her, and her friends, on her rooftop, had been the highlight of his year. She wanted to be friends with him. Simon was so strangely genius; he had headed up his own dot com company that went bust. His looks were purely out of this world, with glow-in-the-dark, platinum, blond hair, and the craziest colour of blue eyes, she had ever seen. He had squandered all his money, and now, was supporting this artist girlfriend, who had never worked a day in her life.

Shirley had commanded his attention at a warehouse rave, where she wore a purple Marie Antoinette mile-high wig, and a very chic, blue dress, with long satin gloves. Her overall look was like a magical princess, and stood out as the most creative of anyone there. She had a knack for that. She had grown into herself as far as having an eye for beauty. Her friends were consulting her more, and more, on what to wear. Her bold choices were lauded, more, and more.

Simon had flown at her virtually out of the blue. The spontaneity of his attraction for her, was what she admired the most about this tryst. He was a compelling looking man, so definitely, she did not have a problem being his fancy. All women love the right kind of attention that comes from a man. The intelligent man will have perfected the flirtation devices that he uses on specific women. There was nothing that Shirley adored more than the subtle charm of an intelligent man. Simon had all of his bases covered when he took her to an outdoor rave in a farmer's field in Chilliwack. She was surrounded by him, and few of his male friends, so she felt very well protected, as the rose amongst the thorns.

Simon had planned the perfect night when his girlfriend was far away on a trip, and took her by the hand in a secluded area, when after restraint on both their parts, gave way to sweet lust out there in the fresh late summer air. Shirley felt like she was a goddess under Simon's gentle caress in this unreal world, that he had built with his divine fervor. She loved it when they arrived home in the wee hours of the morning, after she was dropped off, and only one short hour later, there came a gentle knock on her door.

Simon was full of surprises, he had planned all along this sweet night, when he wanted to show the object of his affections just how wonderful passion could be. He had escaped from his girlfriend to see her, which had been his devious plan after all. The wind had shifted abruptly, when Simon told her that this was to be their private secret, that no one was to know about it. She suddenly felt like a child who had done something that was prohibited, and from the moment he had entered her apartment, she knew the feelings weren't there.

For whatever she got out of this fling, she wanted to remember it for its loveliness, and not for its stupidity, which it really was. She had to give herself more credit than that. Not even this selfish act had served to satisfy her, because at her heart, she knew that was exactly what it was. Being of strong moral fiber got in the way of enjoyment. She couldn't have taken all of the blame in this situation, just some of it, and it didn't take a strip off her at all, because really, she had not played the fool, she had just participated for lack of anything else.

Amongst all his other hollow efforts, Simon had presented Shirley with a copy of "Heart of Darkness." He explained that it had been like reading the story of his upbringing. She was aghast not quite sure what do to with that information, but somehow she felt that he must have had good intentions in her regard. The novel does indeed deal with grave circumstances, so she didn't want to venture to explore exactly that significance, only she knew that Simon had made reference to living on Reserve Land in Crow's Nest Pass, that his father was extremely dysfunctional, which perhaps had something to do with the reasoning.

It was with people new to her life, that Shirley had learned not to pry, when they alluded to the past, she wanted them to unfold their stories to her in a natural way. She, herself was reticent when it came to getting to know people. It wasn't that she was stand-offish, it was just that people would learn more about her, when the time was right. She knew this was all that she would learn about Simon, and with a girlfriend in the wings, she wanted this to be the conclusion. It was a sad thought to be in on the secret about the deceptiveness, which Simon had reflected unto society. The burden of truth was something that many of us as humans have to bear with heavy hearts.

She had really wanted a diversion from Leo, who had always set the regulations, and the boundaries of their ridiculous relationship. Throughout her short affair with Simon, Leo was right there like a chorus in a play, setting the scene, and calling the shots. Shirley's first afternoon with Simon had been spent in the company of Leo, and his friends, on her rooftop, after a night on the town. Leo had orchestrated this set up, his sense of timing was like a wolf's sense of smell.

Leo's voice went up a pitch, and was filled with jealous unnatural tones, when he commented on this surprise visitor. When Shirley had tried to divert her guests to go home, he was incredulous. Simon ended up going home on his own, on that day, She was not able to get a moment alone with him. Leo's friend commented that she wanted to be looked at the way that Simon had looked at Shirley; with the curious adoration that only a man can shower upon a woman.

That was the conundrum for Shirley, her head became dizzy whenever a man gave her that stare. She knew the difference between a disgusting sex stare, and one that was full of loving curiosity. Her dreams would bring on the romantic interludes just like in her favourite soap operas, or she would remember her first love, when the two of them spent the entire day in bed talking endlessly, about their viewpoints. This was a state of delight that she would play over, and over, in her head. She remembered how she went back to the bed the next day, and smelled the sheets, never wanting to let it go.

This was what her, and every woman really wanted, those intense moments when a man isn't doing anything, but giving you his utmost attention. She didn't want all of the material things, she just wanted someone's time once in a while. She was all too sure that she didn't ask for much. Whenever she would whine about it to someone older, and wiser, they would always say, you just have to stop thinking about it, and it will happen.

Control wasn't something that Shirley was familiar with, nor did she really want it. Life was so much more exciting where control wasn't present. Who was that voice of reason anyway? Wasn't she the one who wore a shirt buttoned all the way up to the top of the neck, so that it would choke her, wearing coke bottomed glasses, no make-up, and sensible shoes? There was no use in trying to be something that you couldn't be. She learned, at least to herself, that she couldn't be fooled, but as she became more aware, she knew that presenting a united front to others, was something that she was clever at. There was a sophisticated ease to her, especially in social situations. She was aware of the places that she wanted to be.

Now in her 30s, she wanted to be the one to call her own shots. The severance of the relationship with Leo was much more arduous than she had ever hoped it would be. He was the one who was going to do it, there wasn't a chance in hell that Leo, would let Shirley, be the one to have the final say in the matter. He tore into her soul like a badger in the fight for its' life. She never forgot that last conversation on the phone, when she could hear the receiver at the other end slam like a car ramming into a wall. Desperately, she wanted to give the goodbye some strength, and meaning, but there was no way that Leo would want it that way.

All she could feel was sadness heaving through her veins, and all she wanted to do was to soothe the anger on the other end. She had reasoned this out in her head for months. This wasn't something that she had rushed into with impetuous pride. Her feelings for Leo were tender, and true. No one had filled her up with as many unsurpassed brilliant ideas, ever.

There was a place for everyone who came into our sphere in life. Some people were only meant to be there for a short time, while others were to be there for the duration. She wasn't planning on spending the rest of her life making Leo her, one and only, principal relationship. There was so much damage done to her psyche already in the nine years that she had known him. She did love him, but knew this state of anticipation reminded her of being possessed by suspended beliefs, and definitely was not right for her.

Maybe in the time to come, she would discover what was right, but with her heart in her throat knowing how deeply she cared, was way too much emotive information. This was hurt at its' heightened consciousness. If these feelings that she was having, culminated that hurt that was done, by her participating in this relationship, thus far, the time was long past that she should have let go. Letting go for her should have been easy, after all, she had suffered loss many times in her life. Going through the mourning period was something else altogether.

In the months to follow, that final day, she was a shell of a person looking down upon the remnants of the one who had previously been so full of wonder. There were many tears that she bore witness to, from within herself. Her mind had not chosen Leo, it was her heart. This was not a time in her life that she wanted to be brave, there was no way that she even knew where to begin to be brave, at this moment in time. She had the brain power to do so many things that some people could never do in their lifetimes, but right at this time, she couldn't even hear anything coming from her brain.

All Shirley wanted to do was to be numb, and to go about her day as if she were a drone, to eek out her living as she had always done. If there was a cave that she could live in under a rock somewhere, that is where she wanted to be. The red curtains were tightly drawn in her bedroom, and her head was buried underneath the blankets, as much as possible. Her stomach was dull, her eyes were shut, and her nerves were shattered. She remembered years before, when her Italian dentist pseudo boyfriend had ceremoniously dumped her; how her friends, Debra, and Nina, had dropped in at her apartment, and pried her out of bed.

Shirley was alone now, at this moment, there was not one single person that she wanted to reach out to, because she had just let herself be betrayed by the one person that was entrusted the most. That person was herself. She had led herself to believe that she only needed Leo, and Leo had ensured that there wouldn't be one person left in Shirley's Vancouver family that she could lean on.

There she was to suffer the pain all by herself, and it was her that had let it happen. She had been the one who had let herself fall so deep that she believed all of the lies that she had told herself. She had completely sold out.

Despair did not give way not for years to come, but there were so many conflicting negative voices inside, that she decided to get a professional perspective, to ask for help. Dr. Ann Derks at the downtown medical clinic, had some brilliant connections. Shirley went to see her doctor who immediately set up an appointment with one of the foremost psychiatrists in Vancouver. Dr. Larry had an office on the 30th floor, overlooking Coal Harbour, and it was with great authority that the man of few words, spoke to her with force to shake her at her core, when she needed it the most. Upon pouring out her heart to Dr. Larry, he quickly responded exactly what she needed to do.

Shirley needed to start taking her life seriously, and to stop letting Leo take hold of her in a way that was doing nothing but harm. His sage advice was that if ever she were to see Leo she was to, "Tell him to f**k right off." Just like that, with as much certainty, and gumption as she could muster.

Their sessions where few, but what Dr. Larry had said with punctuation reverberated in her head for times to come, when she needed to feel strong. Not knowing the path that her despair would take in the future, Dr. Larry prescribed some anti-depressants, that made her feel as though she were jumping out of her skin, and some downers, that brought her on to this fluffy plateau.

The uppers were of no use to her, her body chemistry was such that naturally she could vibrate on in a positive cloud, whenever she needed to, these pills made her feel like she was at a rave in the middle of the afternoon, and they had that deluxe time release element that she was hyper-sensitive to. On day three of taking the anti-depressants, the time release high took affect as she was inputting data on to her computer at her boring accounting job. She saw the numbers dancing around on her screen, and felt her breath suddenly becoming more restricted. Later that day, the uppers were thrown into the garbage, but the little blue drowsy ones were put on reserve, in case of an emergency.

The moments of self-degradation, and worry came, and went in waves. Leo had penetrated her soul, and her heart. Logic, therefore, had no place for her, and had become obsolete, whenever she was with Leo. When she wasn't with Leo physically, mentally she was. He was never absent, and when his presence would start to fade, he would with robust fervor, make his entrance.

The despair had won out for many months after the spring of 2002, when she had bade her goodbye to Leo. That wonderful lilac colour that she had worn so many times when she was a teenager, used to make her happy, and cast a glow in her hazel eyes, and olive skin tone. Into the summer months of 2002, all she could think about was dismal black, she couldn't even conjure up a life in colour.

The shadow of losing Leo had made her burst into tears when

she tried to do ordinary tasks. Yoga practice was difficult, especially when meditation time appeared. There was no comfort in going into the fetal position. Everything good just stopped. There were no words that could describe what a person goes through when they experience a loss.

Shirley was so lost, that she had almost been swallowed up into the abyss of no return. Her feelings for Leo were much more powerful that she had ever known. One night after two bottles of wine, she swallowed many prescription downers that she had been given, and although she was apparently engaging in dialogue with her sister for whom she had not spoken to for years, just talking about her serenity at the moment, not fighting the fact that, she was slipping away. She was breathing, her eyes were open but a tranquility that she had never felt before, had taken her above her bodily functions, and she knew that she wasn't afraid.

If Leo and all of his friends had wanted to destroy her, then she, at that defining moment, was ready to let them. It was too much fight, and fury, to go on anymore, when your soul had been swallowed up, and spit out. It was all too much, and the logic had all but disappeared. Her head didn't hurt, her heart didn't hurt, and though she was breathing; that did not even occur to her anymore as some kind of respite, because, it was all just too much. She was not afraid of dying.

Why should we as humans stay around here on earth, just so that others can see to our suffering. Leo was so adept at making her suffer. He didn't even have to say anything to hurt her anymore. She came to for a brief moment, when she realized that there were two policemen staring at her in her apartment, asking her simple questions, such as what is your name? She saw the one officer with the deep contemplative eyes darting around the room, looking at all of the things, as if he were trying to piece together who this woman was, who had tried to die.

Next thing she remembered was the nurse in the emergency department. It was Cindi, Leo's grade school friend looking at her, as if she were speaking for Leo. She knew that Leo would know that she was there in the emergency room, under psychiatric evaluation to ensure she would not succeed in her suicidal sweet surrender. This was exactly how Leo worked his intuitive magic. Of all the duty nurses that had to be on that particular early morning, it just had to be Cindi, whom Shirley had only met a few times in passing.

Leo had bragged that Cindi, was the first woman he had slept with. In the few times that Shirley had met her, she could feel her contempt, and now, again, as fate would have it, she was as vulnerable as she had ever been in her life; with Cindi bearing down on her.

It was times like this that one would refer to as reality being stranger, than fiction. Really, what was the centrifugal force that kept her on this earth. With all of the tribulations she had been through, all that she knew now, was that there was no one for whom she could lean on. All she ever wanted to hear was that everything was going to be alright. That was the only thing that she had ever wanted. She didn't want someone to give her diamonds in the sky. Wasn't it over yet? Why did she have to go through all of this? She had fought back just enough to say that it was too much for her to handle. Why hadn't the powers that be, want to listen to her?

With her central location, she became prey, yet again, to a visitor who she thought was a friend, who suddenly landed on her doorstep from England. Lucy just needed a place to stay while she got oriented from coming back from her life overseas. Shirley obliged, but with this intruder, she could not have foreseen what was to happen.

Lucy who actually told her how much money she had in the bank, took it upon herself to raid her fridge, and steal away one of her new guy friends. What was it about women that makes them so competitive amongst each other? Shirley never could quite understand that some girls wanted to have what she had, and would do everything they could to get it. Out on the town one night, the girls met up with a British bloke named James, who wanted nothing more than to make some friendly connections while he stayed in Vancouver.

Shirley gave her number to James, and two days later, he called her from the lobby of the Pan Pacific Hotel, and said, "Shirley get over here and meet up with me, I am bored." It would take a stupid person to turn down such an offer.

The Pan Pacific had the most stunning lobby lounge that she had ever seen. She had been there a few times throughout the time that she had worked across the street at the Waterford. Well when Lucy got word of where she had been the next day, she was all over that.

The next phone call from James and Lucy was in, at the speed of sound. It was another fun evening with James but later in the night, things just got weird. There came a point when the three of them went back to James' room were jumping on his bed, and drinking some fine champagne. in the drunken haze, she could also see, that James was off in some dark corners making out with Lucy.

So bringing Lucy had ruined it. She knew that this was just a passing through business man, who most probably had a wife, or a girlfriend, or a significant other stuffed away somewhere back in England, and she just wanted to keep it at that.

Some people when they drink, are insufferable they just can't help themselves. They turn into completely different people who will let down their guard enough for others to see what truly motivates them. It was a matter of course, that men can not but help to be led by sex. Women actually thought that sex brought them power.

Shirley felt much more safe when she could decipher that, and participate in a sober context. She resented that this, who was supposed to be her friend, had proven to be so superficial. She had to learn to weed out the superficial people. They came at her like flies to fly paper sometimes.

This particular time she was feeling so exposed, that it didn't take long before she literally turfed Lucy out on her rear. One thing that she was grateful for, was that she still had a difficult time separating people who wanted to do her harm, and those that did not. Why should she have to stoop to their level, and have to think like them?

These kinds of people weren't even worth a thought. It was becoming her mantra, "rise above." She knew the myriad of emotions from her upbringing, with so many siblings, she could feel things just below the surface. It was a blessing that she could have this point of reference. It was just that she had not actually gone through them, but she had been witness to others going through them. Her older sisters and brothers, through their actions, had acted like a fortress. Some emotions that she had were just too scary to emit.

Life would be so much easier if humans didn't have to go through every emotion. Thus far, though, Shirley had thought she could escape some things she was feeling, but at the end of the day, there was no escape, and in the retreat, the emotions only come back like a boomerang.

Love was euphoria, and she just wanted to feel as much of that as she could. She could handle the thought of the existence of extremes, if only from the down, she could be assured to float back up. She was waiting her turn. She was just learning how to swim, but somehow in order not to be crushed, she had to learn how to fly.

Nine: REACHING HOPE, FRIENDSHIP, AND LOVE

Words of Valor: The Aboriginal peoples in Canada know the sacred sacrifices.
The gentle will, is the active guide.
Harm is not to be forgotten.

Like a gentle breeze on her neck, Shirley began to feel life again. In the autumn of 2002, by sheer coincidence, she enrolled in the 2D Design Program, at Emily Carr. There she was in one of her comfort spots, on that man-made island in amongst the artist's studios, the cement factory, and the fresh market; she went to her first classes in formal art.

The inaugural course was, black and white photography. Her instructor was the most amazing man, with a natural expression of beauty, oozing out of every pore. In this world, she had never encountered such a fascinating creature, with eyes like steel, they were so focused, his hands were of the most curvacious shapes, ones that she couldn't keep her eyes off of. There was an aura around this man.

When she would take the little ferry ride home, clear visions of the planes of his face would linger in her mind. It was incredible that someone could have been floating around here on earth, that was supported by the metaphysical void. She sensed that another of her classmates had felt the pull from this man, and engaged in a conversation with Amy, who happened to have her own column in the Georgia Straight. Both girls agreed about this beautiful photographer, when they spoke about him in hushed giggly whispers, that only girls can conjure up, when speaking about their affections.

These feelings were beyond explanations, so Shirley was glad that she had someone to commiserate with. The photography course brought out the best in her. Carte Blanche was given to each of the students to use the dark room, whenever they chose, even into the night. Shirley made her own pinhole camera from scratch, and explored her inner angst, posing herself for an entire self-portrait series. She made her Betty Boop nurse doll, the poster child for cancer, her Ernie doll was dragged on her roof, looking as if he had too much to drink, as she had done so many times before.

The inner whimsical journey had begun without a second thought. She familiarized herself with her inspirations: from the age of 14, her admiration for Thomas Hardy had lit a candle in her head with the flow of his writings; that were the product of his loneliness, his inquisitive nature, and the explorations of the will of man. Through Tess of the D'Uberville's heroine; clearly his viewpoint showed strong women, who were not overshadowed by their hunger for love from a man. It was with meticulous, careful, gentle, detail that Hardy exposed Henchard's weaknesses, in the Mayor of Casterbridge. Henchard was a man, whom Shirley could readily identify, with her own father.

Her strong sense of morality imagined closure for Gideon, much like Henchard had. This man was given the chance to reclaim his love for his daughter; he was given a second chance to tell his child how much he regretted the self destructive decisions he had made, and how much he wanted to love her, as protector. Henchard had been allowed to rise from the ashes, to become a genteel man. This was what she imagined her father would have wanted to do, had he been able to live to even see her through to adulthood. She wanted to hold on to those grandiose images, and probably was right about her father's noble character.

From her soul, she felt immediately akin to Henri Matisse; in his jazz series, she was drawn to the fastidiousness of the lines, and the message in the spirit of the greatest show on earth. His colour palette conveyed outrageously simple choices, meant to wake anyone up, out of their stupor. She couldn't help but to buy the series, and have it shrink wrapped, at her favourite framing shop on Denman Street.

Matisse broke the boundaries of traditions in art, not at all thinking about the literal nature of the world around him. This series of paintings made her buoyant, and full of hope. There was something about them that brought a smile to her face. She didn't even know anything about the artist at all, when she instinctively snatched them up, and brought them home.

Another of her art crushes, was Pablo Picasso, whom she looked up to for not only his fervor for life, but for his bravery to go against the grain, and produce images that were not the norm for his time. Any man who enjoyed his life so much as to parade around wearing various hats, where he could imagine himself in different roles, made her take notice, and stand back to readily admire.

Andy Warhol brightened her eyes with his beliefs in the commercialization of his work; how when he was alive that he was able to live off his art. She could not dispute the beauty of his portrait of Wayne Gretzky with his curly long hockey hair, and the innocence of his face. That was something the Great One never grew too old for, in his face there was this angel, that somehow his wide audience could grasp. Another value that Andy Warhol made known to all of his followers was that he was in love with the concept of celebrities. Shirley too, was absolutely enthralled with this. She would imagine when she was a very young girl, that she was a movie star, and how she would tell the world to be honourable, proud, and to always be grateful for who you are. She would see a great shiny smile come across her face as she shook hands with strangers.

The work that came out of her in the span of eight months from 2002, to 2003, was nothing short of miraculous. There was a series called "Cosmic Sorcery" that explored the world of the metaphysical: "How Do I Reach You?" with wavy, colourful formations, with unexpected hues, intermingled like a collage. This was her first attempt at drawing something seriously, and it couldn't be helped that it resembled some of Henri Matisse works.

The series continued on with, "Exuberant Divinity," that

mirrored a flying powerful entity like Medusa in amongst the stars. "Magnanimous Strength," was her male muse, and appeared to be a medieval king with an overbearingly large crown, and violent scepter. "Recreation of You," showed a sculptor with his tool working on a beautiful woman, with a neck as long as a swan. Her flair for the romantic came out in this particular one; she needed a man with capable hands to be examined by; with a precision in his soul just as this portrait conveyed. "Tranquil Stability," was a portrait of a naked woman being cascaded by a gentle spring of water.

These represented the esoteric dalliances, and morals that she had held so close to her, and finally she had a catalyst to let them come to light. They burst out of her like a fountain of water. The faces all appeared to be wise, serene even, but none of these characters had their eyes open. Was it that one could not bear to delve into the world to really see, and if so what was it that one could not look at? This aura of mystery, was perhaps, what could attract people. The paintings came out in series most likely due to the aspects of her family.

"All the Angels and Saints" was the next in her creative process. She had decided that her spirit animal was a shark, so the Angel-Shark, was the first painting. Her instructor at Emily Carr commented that he liked the dichotomy of it. Shirley had learned that in order to survive in the crazy real world, that she found herself in that she must put up her raw defenses, and looked in wonder at the shark who really was a graceful creature, one that deserved to be at the top of the food chain. She no longer wanted to be metaphorically trampled upon by people, and their hidden agendas. The shark was sure of it's place, and just through observations, one could see the wheels turning in their brains.

She painted: St. Elvis, Prince Angel, St. Betty-Boop, Princess Diana Angel, Saint Ernie, St. Thomas Hardy, St. Mary, and Wolf-Angel. A giant collage of black, and whites pasted on wood, was another piece that she called, "Adios Argentina" on it were images she had remastered from photos she had taken around Buenos Aires. They looked eerie, and ghost like, in 8 x 10s, one of the Casa Rosada, Evita's grave site, the metro train, and the statue in Parque el Centro with the devil tempting a man, amongst others.

The confusing, yet exciting, colourful images were bursting out of her just like the events of her life. She had never really made plans to experience such fascinating things. Events basically fell into her lap, something about her intuitive keenness knew when to climb aboard, to take a chance at life. She had never considered herself a gambler, nor was she ever an opportunist. Her eye for culture was sharp, and her awareness for everything around her was fine-tuned.

Shirley's love for her family for whom she had left behind in Ontario for twelve years at this point had suddenly called to her attention, in July 2003. In November 2002, Shirley had been called by her sister Sheila, who was diagnosed with breast cancer.

Sheila was 44 years old, one of the middle children in the family. She had distinctive images of her experiences with Sheila as a teenager. Sheila worked at a shoe store, had bought a 1975 burgundy Camaro, and wore a burgundy leather jacket to match. As a little girl, she would look at her older sister in admiration, and was privileged to drive around with her in that powerful machine. Sheila had forged her way through life by working very hard, at whatever job she had.

She remembered that her sister had worked at Tim Horton's, at Maher Shoes, and then at Bowe's Publishers, for over 20 years. Her sister had endured many tough times in her marriage to a man five times the size of her, who abused her, and finally when Sheila decided to leave, she felt a sense of pride in herself once more. She was free, and had met a man who wanted to help her realize her dreams.

The news of Sheila's diagnosis was met by Shirley with shock, in fact for months, she was in denial, and told herself that there were so many break through treatments in our modern times, that she was optimistic that her beloved sister would pull through.

Sheila was a special phenomenon in that this was a woman who had a high threshold to pain, much like Shirley did. It was no easy task for Sheila to reach out for help when she needed it. The cancer had relentlessly taken her sister, who was not one to make a ruckus about anything. Shirley remembered the humour she had shown, when she had made the final decision to end her tumultuous marriage. She announced this to her little sister, as if it was a matter of fact, that she had mulled over in her head with calm, reserve.

She was besotted with her grief. She was called to return to London at the height of the death vigil for her sister. The memories were things that no one could take away. Shirley was lucky enough to have Sheila visit Vancouver in 2001, all on her own, with no children, or husband. The short, but sweet, visit was just what she needed, at a time in her life when she too, was going through loneliness, and was retreating from the world, except for her relations with Leo. After briefly meeting Leo, who had interfered with Shirley's alone time with her sister, all that Sheila had to say was, "He's short." This was her way of calling her little sister out. It's like this, "I call them as I see them."

Shirley then showed Sheila the sights of Vancouver, taking her to the Amsterdam Cafe. Sheila in all her innocent, charm, blurted out, "I can't get over it, here we are, and I'm looking at this guy sitting in this beautiful Victorian space, with an elegantly, grand cup of tea, smoking a joint." There probably was no where that she had been that was so civilized. In her sweet joking manner infused with her melodic way of speaking, Sheila spoke sporadically all day about the many uses of hemp.

In retrospect, this time with her sister would always be dear to her. Sheila had a message to give Shirley, she felt that her little sister would not truly be aware of her potential in life, and meet the man of her dreams, until she was older. She listened to her half-hardheartedly, not really wanting to hear that she would have to wait.

This was one of her defense mechanisms, to block out the things that she probably needed to hear, but really didn't want to hear. Sheila wanted to give her little sister a sweet token of affection before she left, and gifted Shirley with a candle in the shape of a turtle. That little sentimental object stayed near and dear to her heart, for years into the future.

Love was really what bound us together; sisters were meant to stand beside one another no matter what came to pass. These values quiet unexpectedly came to a head with the impending death of her sister, the first yet to occur of all her siblings. There was nothing else as pure as love.

Not to be overshadowed Shirley's sister Carol had also been diagnosed with breast cancer and was having her own battle at the very same time. The family unit was shook to the core with a jostling of devastating ailments.

In the middle of July 2003, her plane touched down in Toronto, Ontario at 9:30 at night. She was quickly whisked away from the airport from her brother George, who drove like a bat out of hell. In fact, everything that George did was at hyper-speed. Without having time to truly absorb the severity of the situation, George told her that she would be dropped off at the palliative care ward of the hospital to spend the whole night there alone with her sister

Sheila, who the doctors knew, did not have long to live.

She was not really too sure what to expect at all. The communicative chain between her and her other siblings, was not so clear. There were so many complicated personalities all vying for attention. At the crisis point, she found that mainly the bulk of her siblings, behaved quite badly.

She was grateful to have a birds-eye perspective, but had heard that there were so many visitors to Sheila's bed side that the nurses on the ward had to cut down the visitors, to one at a time. She was not present herself, but through many different tirades from her sisters, pieced together the picture. What really must have happened was that the sisters must have argued right there on the palliative ward enough to make the nurses put up their defenses, to enforce some rules.

There were too many people yelling, and arguing for attention in her clan, and not enough people who could calmly give perspective. This was a large family who knew each other well, who communicated with passion, and often times there were those who just simply did not get along.

So Shirley was thrust into the fray, as the over night vigilante at her dying sister's bedside. That was always her role that even though distance and time was between her, and her family, she knew it so well. She would be subjected to all kinds of clashes of opinion, to strong personalities, and would have to wade through them all to decide just what she thought.

In this instance, however, it was trivial. She had visited with Sheila four months prior, and was able to ascertain just how far along the disease had gone. It had caused a huge gauge in her body, where the breast was operated on, right to the bone. Sheila couldn't eat properly through the rounds of radiation treatments, and her finger nails were cracked so severely, that they were barely there.

Shirley had been called upon by her other sisters, to spend what little time she had, and was only able to spend one night, at Sheila's home. The air there was thick with tension, as her second husband came right out, and told her, that he hesitated to let her stay, because he thought she was too rowdy. Yes, Shirley had to admit that she could cause quite a stir, but it was all just a release mechanism that she had in her way of dealing with the pressures of all of the information she would receive from her siblings, all at once. She wondered though how this man could be so inflexible knowing that her visits were so short, and were spread out through at least five years, at a time. All of this didn't matter now. Here, in July 2003, she was just so grateful that she would be able to spend these last hours, with her dear sister.

The hospital room was not private, in fact, there was a man right next to Sheila, moaning, and groaning all night. Shirley sat by the bed in a haze of silence trying to piece together what it must be like for her sister, who was so close to death. Sheila would be in, and out of consciousness. When she came to, she would ask

Shirley to stay there, she said she was afraid of being left alone, and asked over and over, if she was going to die.

Asking about the inevitability, at such a time, profoundly hit close to Shirley's emotions. She answered her sister as well, and as honest, as she could. She said, "We're all going to die." Sheila wanted Shirley to know that the doctors were killing her. The sight of her once bright-eyed, smiley, bubbly, sister laying there with her head completely bandaged, and one eye with an eye patch took its toll on her, but she remained dignified. She needed to keep steady her composure, because that is exactly what was called for, and appropriate to the occasion.

There is no greater force than the human will, especially when we want to live. Her sister definitely wanted to live. Sheila was aware of Shirley's wild sense of fun, and at times that night, would poke fun at the fact that she had $5000 worth of orthodontic work just done, "It sucks. Your teeth are so nice." She said. In these moments, Shirley could see that light in her eye, that she wanted to capture, right there, and never let go. It was only a week later, that Sheila died there, at the hospital. The second oldest of the family, Brenda was right there the moment it happened. The room was crowded, and there they all were, giving this body a farewell, one that had been punished beyond what anyone would have to endure, in their life time.

She was so sad, but she knew that the pain was gone. On that night, July 29, 2003, Shirley looked up into the sky, and saw a shooting star, writing Sheila's name in the sky. This is, but a brief stop that we have, along the journey of life. If there was a heaven, Shirley was glad to let her sister go there. Sheila had trusted people that didn't deserve her trust. She was taken away so that she wouldn't have to be subjected to the grief, and stress, of being surrounded by the wrong people.

The funeral was hollow for her; the body was cremated immediately. It had never been a tradition in her family previously, to not at least have a viewing, at the wake, before the funeral. In some weird way it gave loved ones a sense of finality, and let's face it, those funeral directors certainly know what they are doing. Those bodies that are laid out for viewing, look fabulous, and they have a way of making the person wear a peaceful expression on their faces.

Ah, eternal rest from the dread of this mad world. She loved the body state of sleep. What an amazing invention that was! One could feel reborn after a full, restful sleep. Shirley just knew inside that her sister may feel turmoil to worry about her children who were so young, her son was 18, and her daughter 12. Sheila had a way with her children, that reflected friendship at its most, its truest. She remembered after she had married her first husband, and saw her older sister having babies, that she cried, she wanted children so much.

Sheila indeed felt blessed to be a mother. When people need to rise to the occasion to do what they must, it works out just fine.

Nothing on earth, though, can replace the love that a mother has, for her child. This is a mysterious force that fortifies humanity. Shirley was fine with death, early exposure to that fact of life, had made her almost comfortable with the thought. It wasn't a big mystery after all, every person will have to experience death.

One thing that lingers beyond death, is the manner in which you, as a person, had made the people around you, feel. That is what is remembered, and all of us as individuals, have a duty to make people feel good. Sheila made Shirley feel good; she knew that Sheila had felt on equal terms, even though she was just her little sister. The sound of her beautiful, soprano voice, would ring true forever, and those big eyes that laughed, would burn in her mind.

Death could not take the essence of her sister away. She was so privileged, she knew, to be the youngest of such a large family. She was able to truly know so many people, and let them give her pieces of themselves. We are truly having a humanizing experience, with family. When you needed their help; they were there.

Going back to Vancouver, felt much different at the end of that summer. She was ready to move on with the job that she had. Her boss was quite judgmental, and had the audacity to accuse her of staying in London too long. Shirley knew that her boss was suspicious of the reasons why she had stayed as long as she had to, even though, Shirley told her, that her sister was dying. Top priorities in life were shifting. She grew tired of having to convince those around her of her sincerity. It didn't resonate with the kind of person that she wanted to be.

She had seen what destruction was possible by having the wrong people in close quarters. Princess Diana, was another prime example to her. This was a woman that had everything, yet nothing at all. She didn't want to be that way, so she quit her comfortable job as accounting assistant, at one of the largest, and oldest printers, in Vancouver. This was a tough decision, yet she knew that no matter how hard she tried, the job just didn't match her, at all. It was sad though, truly as the building must have been a landmark, at one point, and it was located only a few blocks away from one of the most important places in Vancouver, in Shirley's estimation; Granville, Island.

Like every decision she had made in the past, she went full tilt like jumping from an airplane, with no parachute. This vibrant 30 something, was ready for whatever was ahead. This may have meant having to take a job that was beneath her capabilities, but that was something Shirley was accustomed to, and she was ready to roll with it. She didn't let herself down though, and was pleased when, she was given an assignment at a prestigious doctor's office, that was affiliated with the provincial government. It had to be one of the most simple jobs, yet she was able to have the inside view of what it was like to work side by side, with doctors.

These specialists had so much paperwork, and she was able to listen in on their appointments. It was gratifying to her to have that contact, and to know why doctors, especially in Canada, have so much pressure on them. This was Shirley in her element, being able to fill in, wherever she was needed, at that office. With gusto, she took on assignments that the other clerks thought were beneath them. Filing was no chore at all to her. She knew, however, that this was a temporary assignment, but in the end was able to drag it out for over a year. It was so sad for her when that job ended. For the first time in her life, she was actually making money, and making a difference in people's lives.

There was no looking back over her shoulder. During this time, her personal life seemed empty, except for her full participation in her art. She was now painting shark portraits on canvas, using a highly toxic paint, she devised a method of painting clear paint on mirrors, that had the reflective effect, that mimicked stained glass. There was no where that her imagination didn't want to go. Her energy outside of work was boundless. The seawall visits were frequent, and she even employed roller blades to get her around. She would pick up the Georgia Straight, every Thursday, and sought out the best art exhibit openings in the city. This was where she would meet new people.

She was always challenging herself with art, going so far as to buy a violin, picking up on her childhood where she was lucky enough to be part of an orchestra in her primary school. She was bursting with ideas, and growing in all directions. Met with adversity, as she did in her life, she had to seek another job, which was this time, much more difficult than it had seemed before. It may just be a matter of luck, or it was just a matter that for a woman with so many skills, her place in the job market was slipping down a slippery slope.

When she had to set aside all of her pride, there she was at the end of 2004, having to take a job in a call centre. What dread she had hanging over her head day in, and day out. Her mind had become some sort of cheap commodity, and her soul was slipping away with each day that she worked there. Forever the resourceful person that she was, she managed to find a way to make this assignment tolerable, and discovered that she would be able to use the company gym, without extra cost. Shirley was there exercising as much as possible. It was certainly a wonderful bonus, somewhat of a gift, that was given to her, to get her through.

Something else quiet unexpected was also brewing behind her in the background, at this time, and that was a love interest. This one came at her like a title wave right out of the clear blue sky. The influence that this brief; but sparkling love affair would have on her, could not be measured. Shirley was there doing something that her heart, nor her head, nor her soul, wanted to participate in, but she was not alone, no, not in the least. At this place of employment, she found two birds of a feather.

Tatiana presented herself to her as if they had known each other from many by-gone days, with an effervescent, strange, yet hilarious wit. The two of them would come out with the strongest statements about reality, that Shirley had once again found her partner in crime. The place of business was no place for the fun that the two of them conjured up, and what great costumes they came up with at work for Halloween, the office did not even know what had hit them.

The unexpected was occurring, and unfolding, for her once again. This was led on by her heightened sense of fun. She was like a kid, and the one-liners rolled off her tongue, like no other time in her life. She now was a full adult, with all of her sophisticated faculties to match. The loud pair of traveling comedians were a welcome distraction for Aristotle, whom also worked at this strange, yet social work place. Ari, was smitten by the friendships that slapped him in the face like cold water. He could not help, but to be attracted to the sense of fun that Shirley and Tatiana emanated, from their beings.

Ari was like the air, in that he would take people in, and this pair of insufferable women, were just too hard to resist. He wanted to be in this fellowship of raucousness. The days were just spent making the most of the barren life that Shirley had made for herself at her home. On Saturdays, in the morning, she volunteered at the Contemporary Art Gallery. The exhibits were second to none, and she was astonished by the artists.

One particular group, were a team of performance artists, from Austria. She was in her pleasure zone, when she worked their opening. The artists staged a mock burial, for which the audience was able to be active in. They played this staid musical anthem, and an audience member carefully stepped into a pine coffin, and closed the lid. The artists proceeded to throw dirt over the coffin, while the crowd gathered around, and observed.

She was there to be a silent observer, only that was her role, because while there, she sensed that she was yet again, an outsider, looking in to the family gathered around at the dinner table. The proprietor of the gallery would shuffle by her with a look of indignation, as if what she were doing there had no significance whatsoever. Therefore, the emotional exchanges that were being brought forth to her from this current job, were much more than just people put together in circumstances, because they had to be. She felt the force of her own needs, so much so, that this employment, and the people she worked with, meant everything to her.

Shirley was a fool in amongst people who were just nice to her, because they had to be and besides, it made their grueling job, much more bearable. She was fooled once again by the affections of her potential suitor, Fernando. Fernando was the type of guy for whom she wouldn't even have given a second look, if he hadn't pursued her.

Suddenly, after a break at work, outside on the street, he walked right up to her, and told her passionately, how classy she looked. She could feel her feet rise above the ground, instantly. It was magnificent that a man would, with natural agility, pay her such a sincere compliment. She was gone just like that, bam!

Their short but sweet love affair culminated into some soap opera scenes of passion that of course Shirley wanted to believe, so badly. Tatiana could see the folly of her foolish mindset toward this Mexicano, and gently tried to talk her out of her love addiction.

Shirley heard only the things that she wanted to hear. Fernando relished feeding her, only the things that he knew, she wanted to hear. His words would come back to haunt her a year into the future, but at the time of their meeting, it was as if she were hypnotized. Shirley made glory out of the impossible. It was pure, honey the things that this Mexicano man would say. Fernando called her one day on her cell phone while she was walking around the seawall at the height of their tryst. He played his classical Spanish guitar into the phone, and said after, that he was just thinking about her. A serenade, how unreal was that? Just what was that? What movie had Fernando taken that out of? The charade was unbelievable, and to the onlooker with their brain attached to their body, they would be able to see the absurdity in it.

Like a repeated scene from a bad movie, she was sick when Fernando suddenly announced that he was moving to Guadalajara, Mexico, where he had a dream to run his own business. She wanted this dream of hers to last as long as it could. She was besotted. With tremors inside, and fear worn on her face, she spent her final night with her lover, at a social gathering that included his family, and Tatiana. Just what zombie medicine had Shirley taken that she felt that the impossible, was possible, no one could imagine.

Six months into the future in May 2005, she was on an airplane to Guadalajara, Mexico with high flying romantic dreams, that her and Fernando, would be reunited once more. Again, as before, in her life she did not have a plan mapped out, she just went with the air that she breathed, and hoped that it would see her through.

The trip lasted only five days during which she had to plead, fight, and cry to be with Fernando. The romantic, say-anything Mexicano, was in total shock that this daring Canadian would pursue the relationship further than he had wanted it to go. In her hotel room, Shirley was, for most of the visit, alone. Upon landing in the metropolis she was over taken by the smells of the sixteenth century sewage system, the heaps of garbage lining the crumbling streets, and of the dissonance of her, as a figure, who stood out amongst the throngs of people.

She was able to visit some of the beautiful sights of the city, and was overwhelmed by fear, that she was alone. If she were using her brain at all, she wouldn't have gone back, but at the end of the initial visit; as much as people are unpredictable, they can be predictable as well. Fernando ran into her arms on the day she left, and promised, he would change, that he was sorry, and that he loved her. What the two of them had together, was in his words,

"Something else." This was the type of manipulative tools that Fernando had in his arsenal of words, that he knew was all that he needed to say, in order to make Shirley linger. It was just like a cat, and a mouse. Retrospectively not such a good idea after all.

Ten: ANOTHER DECADE, ANOTHER COUNTRY

Words of Valor: It's one of those, 'what was I thinking?' moments.
When I opened my eyes, I saw a bright, shiny light.
To go beyond one's capabilities. is sometimes
disadvantageous.

Shirley could be a worthy adversary to any intellectual, but when it came to love, she was like a child, so wanting to be free of her loneliness, that intellect was completely shunned, for the need to believe was far, stronger, than her mind could fight against.

With very little of her personal dignity in romance intact, once again she made the perfect specimen. She talked herself into moving to Guadalajara, and went online in search of a certification program, for teaching English as a second language. She was on to her next challenge like a pure bred horse chomping at the bit, ready to race. Really, hadn't this woman been born ready? Was it that much of a stretch for her to pack up all of her belongings, give away most of them, and move to a country thousands of miles away? Her values changed all the time, and deciding on what was best for her, wasn't in the hands, of anyone. She was, at her core, an independent thinker. She knew the score, she had done it before in Buenos Aires, and besides, she would remind herself, that she really had nothing to lose, and everything to gain.

The articles were sold, the one-way flight was arranged, and the English teaching course, was booked. Would other people take such risks? Probably not, but this was a unique person, who had proven all along her complicated path, in her journey of life, that she was capable of such revolutionary measures. It was with a certain kind of savvy then, that she landed in Guadalajara, on September 16, 2006. She became a member of the lonely hearts club, immediately when she got there. Fernando had no intention of living up to the promises he had made. Knowing that there was no turning around to go back, to her sterile existence in Vancouver, she took in the sights in the downtown core of Guadalajara, which was littered with party favours, and people were everywhere, to celebrate the Mexican, Independence Day.

This was an insular society, most people who lived in this city were of Mexican descent. Shirley was an anomaly as a Canadian woman, and she wanted to stand out, because by this point in her being, that was where, she was comfortable. She wasn't one to brag, but she had certainly earned the right to. A woman from such a humble background, would not have the stories that she would have to tell, at the end of her days. Seize the moment, she told herself in the sweltering heat, on that first day.

Guadalajara, was the de facto, real, Mexican city. It had survived the 16th century revolution, in tact, with its domed buildings, and most obviously by the smell, its sewage system, as well. The downtown streets were cobble stoned, and lined with government buildings, from that era. The domed buildings were still used in an official capacity. It was an arid climate, the city was well above sea level, with the median temperatures at about 25 degrees Celsius, all year round. The shops were very mom and pop traditional, with all of them being run, as a family business.

Commercialization had only spread into the outskirts, as was evident from the posh, elaborate malls. She would go to these malls when she felt that she needed a dose of Canada. Wherever you walked, in the downtown core, you would come upon dozens of open kitchens with people standing around eating wholesome, simple, fresh, market food. One of the largest open markets Shirley had ever seen was the San Juan, which was a cornucopia of goods. There in that one, run down, dilapidated, loud, bustling, dirty place; one could buy just about everything.

From her standpoint, even though all of the goods were cheaply made, they all possessed a cheerful, soulful beauty, that was so pleasing to the artist's sensibilities. Each item of clothing even if it were a designer rip off, told a story. There was a rare point of reference, for her to compare the Latino culture of Argentina, with the Latino culture of Mexico. Mexicans wore there hearts on their sleeves. They were innocents. The Mexicanos embraced their indigenous roots, to the extent that they were proud of them. They didn't try to hide the fact that many of them were not rich. The Argentines were a master at that disguise.

They didn't try to be anything else, then the best of what they could be. Within this setting, she knew she could manage great things, even alone. Perhaps it was better that she was alone after all. She was willing to try at this point, she really had no choice, for she had removed herself from reality, so far beyond any, that she had done before. It was never easy to live in these types of circumstances where the true defining changes were not even contemplated. She audaciously did things, and then she would just hope for the best.

Some of the greatest minds had proven to the world that stepping outside what is considered normal, may be distressful in the short-term, but came with many rewards, for the long-term. This was, in essence, what Shirley had conceived in her mind, she did have a goal, and that was to turn around her career chances. She knew that she would return to Vancouver, but she would return far richer for her experience in Mexico, or so she wanted to believe.

Being an English teacher in the heart of Mexico was no small undertaking. She was in a class with twenty other, mostly American, twenty-somethings, who had just graduated from college, and were looking for adventures. In contrast, she was ten years older, and was the only Canadian in the group. This was only irritating to some of the classmates, who were clearly taken aback by the perceptions, and the inspirations, that only a Canadian perspective could reflect.

This was a Canadian girl, with her increasingly liberal, democratic ideals. She had only considered herself mildly political before her time there, with introspection during this time, she developed a distinct political bend to her personality. By engaging in conversations with the locals, she knew that the people in Mexico had felt that same kind embarrassment, towards the solipsistic characteristics, of Americans; who indulged in their urge even toward their neighbours.

Many of the educated Mexicans were complicit, in this understanding, of what it was like to be shadowed by the American empire. Many of the images of Mexicans, that she had seen in the popular media, had belied the true nature, of the culture. She had felt this kinship early on, but at the same time she was exposed to many very sexually aggressive Machismo attitudes. She found their advances brazen, and offensive. She didn't even want to give them leeway, or hear the excuses, such like, that they were from the lower classes, and therefore uneducated.

Socially, by Shirley's estimation, people should conduct themselves with some degree of decorum. This uncouth, sordid behaviour, on the part of many of the men in Guadalajara, towards women, made her skin crawl. She didn't paint all of them with the same brush, however, and found some fascinating men in the crowds. Occasions came when she would meet attractive, almost innocent, Mexican men. Her roommate, and she, met two such boys who were from Sinaloa, the drug capital of Mexico. She of course was oblivious to this fact, and was eager to learn the traditional dances of the different regions of the country. One such dance movement was known as the country dancing called, "Banda."

She was to discover an underworld of clubs where Banda was king, with it's music; where couples would grind up against one another. The women would be swung into the air. There was something so erotic, yet coarse in their movements, that she couldn't get enough of. It was like Dirty Dancing, but with less elegance. The typical band of Mariachi men were so intriguing, and when they sang about how pathetic their love lives were, Shirley couldn't help but find them a bit comical with their tight studded pants.

But she could not deny the universal appeal of the music, with massive bands, with just about every type of brass instruments, there, on one stage, lined up with more than a dozen men. She had not expected the proportions of the beats, on the thick guitars, and the thumping of their feet, with the enormity of the passions, conveyed in their voices. This was a show to be reckoned with, the reflections of the culture showed deeply in this entertainment. The Mariachis wandered alone through markets, and outdoor restaurants, but the group shows were the best. There was no standard by which Shirley could have measured their music.

Teaching at the largest institute in Guadalajara, was all encompassing. The bulk of her days were spent engaging with her students. She was lucky enough to have an array of students from various backgrounds. Most of them were university aged, but a sprinkling of them were teens, or pre-adolescents. Her teaching schedule was grueling, to put it mildly. Classes started at 9:00

a.m., and went until 9:00 p.m., with three hours in between for lunch, and siesta. On Saturdays every week, she conducted two classes, one was from 9:00 a.m. to 2:00 p.m., and the last class of the day was from, 3:00 p.m. to 6:00 p.m.

This was the proverbial, ultimate teaching ground. It was like boot camp, or being a teacher, on steroids. She was able to forge some lifelong friendships through her time there. The school ran under strict discipline. At any given time, in any given class, Shirley was observed by the principal of the school. Under a great deal of duress, during the very first lessons, she had to command classes of up to 25 students, and she wasn't allowed to let them see her sweat. In the months that followed, she eventually became at ease, and unquestionably more competent.

Outside of the classroom, there were rumblings going on, that Shirley could not have conceived. The class that she had graduated from, were the first class of foreigners hired, at this long-standing, English institution. She was not aware that she would be part of these testing grounds. Nothing was communicated to her, that they would be paid at a wage that was higher. She would be in the crowded break room every day, with her colleagues, who behind her back, resented her.

It wasn't as if the wage that she made was substantial at all, in fact, she made the equivalent of $6.00 an hour Canadian. It was with favour, that she was looked upon, especially by the son of the owner of the school, that caused the greatest disdain. Months into working there, one day unexpectedly out of nowhere, there appeared this willowy figure of a man, at the port hole door of her classroom.

Shirley went to the door to see what he wanted. This was Jorge, the school masters son. He asked Shirley to work with him for two hours per day, on a special assignment as writer of all of the promotional materials, for the school. She was swooning, though she had to recover to continue with her class. The students were more than communicative. Their hot-blooded passions were just below the surface. As a teacher, Shirley found it easy to get them to speak. The most difficult part of her role, was to teach four different levels, in one class. There wasn't an equal level of comprehension in any of her students. Their abilities, and strengths, had to be measured with great care.

She became cognizant of the inequities, as she matured into her career. It was a balancing act to be sure. A teacher had to be aware of the functionality of the language in this particular setting, whereby students didn't have the opportunities to speak English, outside the classroom. She was fiery in her attainment of understanding. The opportunities abounded as she was called on to take more responsibilities, within such a large institution. She missed a total of a day, and a half, of work, in the entire year and a half, that she worked there.

Her loyalty was fierce. This was a job that her intellect could grapple with. The grammar lessons were the most enjoyable, because she found a universal methodology, and used musical rhythm, to dispel the gloominess of the task. Some of her younger students would belt out the songs, and cause quite a loud ruckus throughout the school. Shirley became known by her beautiful housewives group, for the dance sessions they would engage in, when over the loud speaker, the song of the day would signal the end of each class. "Every Breath You Take!" They all knew the words.

She had struck a balance between learning, and celebrating life. It was no wonder, then, as time went on, that resentments from her colleagues, became apparent. She was one of the survivor foreigner contingent, and it must not have been expected, that she would last there, as long as she had.

Like all endeavors, there does come a time when negativity slowly creeps in, no matter how hard we try. We all have a dark shadow. She had managed to keep her two hour position, with the head of research and development, for a year. This was a much coveted position, and with more foreign teachers coming and going, some of them would wonder, if they would ever get the chance.

Through conversations with the dashing Jorge, she revealed her love for art, and the fact was, that she had brought her work with her. Jorge jumped at the chance to promote this special Canadian, with whom he had taken quite a liking to, in the course of their time working together. He arranged a showing of all of Shirley's art in the auditorium of the school. Months previously, she had managed to get the word out that she had brought her art, and was invited to take part in an exhibition at the downtown gallery: "Casa de Los Perros." This stately marble arched building, had its own historical significance. The story was, that the gallery used to be the mansion of an eccentric millionaire in the 1920s, who had immortalized his dogs, who now graced the second floor of the edifice, looking down at the front of it, to guard the house, for all eternity. Legend had it, that in the dead of night, the dogs were said to move. and switch sides.

It was a beautiful gallery, and she was commissioned to take part in the exhibit, whose theme was postcards from around the world. Shirley rendered two post card sized paintings to represent, Eastern Canada, and the other to represent, Western Canada. She painted an outline Hudson's Bay, a beaver, and a hockey stick, on one post card, and on the other, a silhouette of Queen Elizabeth, an indigenous ceremonial mask, and the mountains. This was her debut, amongst other artists, who drew politicized phrases, with blood, and gore. This was truly what it meant to be Canadian. One who could appreciate the beauty of her surroundings, and be proud of the multicultural heritage, that was undeniably, peaceful.

Canadians essentially deplored bloody revolutions. She was impressed by her country's almost, spotless reputation, and became to realize just what it was, to have a government, who was for the most part, for the people. In Mexico, there existed this shadow over it's citizens when the topic of their government came up.

From the time that she first moved there, she could see the abject poverty that most of the people had to live under, whereas, what would be considered the middle class people, who worked their fingers to the bone, just to live from pay cheque to pay cheque. They had no trust in banks, in the police, and security was principally found, through their families. When it came down to any discussion about their political leaders, most Mexicans were apathetic. They were despondent, as corruptible forces had infiltrated the very fabric of society, so deeply, that there really was, no way out.

They found no use in trying to rail against injustice. One of her students who was a lawyer, protected her from the loathsome treatment, she had faced from being a renter. The margin of rental spaces in Guadalajara, was slim to none, and were only there for those, who were desolate. Most of the local people lived with their families. She grudgingly found herself having to move on four different occasions. It was as though landlords in Guadalajara, had invented the term "slum landlords." One morning, to her dismay, she came upon the largest, and ugliest, rat crawl across her kitchen counter. This instance, was one of such shock, and horror, that one could never have imagined it, not even in nightmares.

With so much intimacy with the Mexican culture under her belt, all the good, bad and the ugly, the time was ripe for her to think about getting back to her homeland. Time spent there had fortified her belief, that there was no price on freedom. During the most dramatic exchanges, and two brushes with death, it was time for her to figure out how she was going to get back to Vancouver.

She had been thrown from a taxi as it was speeding to escape, after the driver had robbed her of fifty dollars, and in broad daylight, she was accosted by a strange man, who with great force, lifted her skirt, with both his hands. After these two blows to her perceptions of humanity, and knowing that she had exposed herself enough, to the dangers there were in Mexican society; it was time.

During the year and half, that she lived there, she was able to visit a kindred spirit of hers who had been drawn to her from the first day of her class at the teaching institute, who resided in Puerto Vallarta. The force of the bond that she had with her friend Abby, comforted her weary soul.

She was to fly from Puerto Vallarta, back to Vancouver, and Abby the unassuming free spirit from Iowa, would ensure that she would have a grand send-off. The year before, Shirley took the bus during Holy Week finally, to see the best of the Mexican culture, that was along their immense coastlines. The beaches there were so pristine. She falsely had imagined that the coast would be much like the city. This was the finest part of life in Mexico.

After meeting all of Abby's friends, and going to high end clubs there in the resort town, Abby booked a whale watching tour. The booze cruises were commonplace for locals. Lunch was prepared on the boat and drinks were in constant supply. The tour was not short on adventure, when it made a stop along a shallow reef, the sight seers, were invited to snorkel dive. She was so bogged down with her job, that she wasn't prepared for the amazing time that she had. She certainly was grateful, but Abby had more surprises in store for that week. There was a friend, of a friend, of hers, that made the plastic bracelets, that people needed to wear, to enter all-inclusive resorts in Nueva Vallarta.

This area of the town was exclusively owned by large hotel chains. As the two of them drove up in the taxi, wearing their bracelets, both of them were a typical sight there, with their long blonde hair, and fashionable sunglasses. They walked through the lobby as if they owned the place, and planted their towels on chase lounges, and plunged into the pool, with the swim up bar.

Shirley went to the bar, and ordered not one, but two drinks. Abby questioned why she ordered two, and to which she answered, "Because I can." They spent the day there drinking by the pool, at dinner they went to the buffet dinner that was miles long, and at night, they stayed to watch the show. This was the excitement that she could have had, but no, she took the long way around, when she decided to slug it out in landlocked, Guadalajara.

She felt disillusioned into thinking that she was privileged to have, such a great career opportunity. She was beyond exhaustion, when finally, she came to her last days in Mexico. She wouldn't be sad about leaving. There was no way that she could look back upon the experience with regret. She had participated fully in all that she could, while she was there. Her students only said,"We don't know why you want to leave." They would miss this special, crazy Canadian woman. Shirley was wound up on her last night on the town with Abby, and friends. It was as the phrase goes, "Going out on a high note." Shirley and Abby, jumped out of bed almost too late to catch the plane. With her tousled hair, and suitcases that must have weighed half a metric tonne, the pair stopped briefly at a taco stand, so that Shirley could get her last meal on the run.

The tradition was to stand there on the street, and eat whatever you could fit in your stomach, with your choice of meats such as tongue, and an array of fresh toppings that always included fresh cilantro, and lime on top. Everything tasted better with a fresh squeeze of lime. She was allowed to get on the plane hassle free, much to Abby's surprise, without having to pay for the obviously grossly, overweight bags.

She was grateful in the end, and with a slight bit of temerity, was ready to reemerge on to Canadian soil, once again. This time she would return with a renewed sense of pride in being able to pursue a career path, that she hoped would go a long way towards solidifying a prosperous future. She felt a calm sense of inner pride in her country through a perspective, that was much more palpable than the one she had experienced, in Argentina.

Shirley had gained many friends in Guadalajara. The principal of the school called her into his office on her last day there, and told her, "You have many friends here." Jorge had stood up from his desk, and they embraced warmly, for minutes. Shirley had actually witnessed a living, breathing attestation, to the man she had envisioned, since she was a little girl. She could not help to feel like jello inside whenever she was around him.

She would make joking dramatic remarks, to Jorge's right hand man, when he would leave the office. Shirley was sure she was going to die. One of her portraits of a wizard, called, "No Blood for Oil," with a long dark beard, resembled Jorge. It was as though she had known of his presence before, as this ethereal magical wizard, who would elegantly enter, and exit, her life. Jorge had the mannerisms of a true gentleman, and when all was said and done, she knew that somewhere deep in his soul, he had been watching out for her as a guide, in his own quiet way. She had needed someone who would watch over her like a sentinel, and she only shed a tear of joy, of knowing that he had been there.

It was March of 2008, and Shirley had touched down at, Vancouver International Airport, another time, without incident. What a life she had so far, so much more was left. The internet had made it possible for Shirley to arrange an accommodation through one of her friends from the call centre. Shaunalea was a beautiful red head, with a beautiful soul. She was so grateful to have such a person on her side. She found a place in East Vancouver, in the upstairs of a home, shared with a girl, who lived in the downstairs.

It wasn't the desirable neighbourhood, of west of Denman, but Shirley was determined that again, she would make Vancouver home. It wasn't long before she realized, that she had mingled, with the wrong type of people. The next few years, in fact, seemed like a series of tough knocks, to her. Perhaps she was just in the wrong place, at the wrong time.

The house she had moved into, had gone through some turmoil, and there were too many people, who drank too much alcohol, around, all of the time. There was no denying, however, that Shirley looked smashing. All of the work she had done in Mexico had shown in her face. She was thin, svelte even, from the fresh diet, the polluted water, and the pursuance of her job. Her forty year old body looked thirty. With her bustling schedule, she really didn't have time to eat. Tatiana had expressed it when she saw her, how something must have agreed with her.

Maybe it was because she was in the presence of a gentleman every day, and also wanted to present her best self, in front of the students. Whatever it was, it involved enrichment. That was the mantra of many people who are successful. Even if circumstances turn out to be difficult, there is always a trace in that process, that serves to make us better. She would have to hang on to that concept for the next two years, because the series of events, which took place from early 2008, to early 2010, knocked her off her game, so to speak.

The reemergence culture shock that she was to face, shook her to her core.

With the instance, at her East Vancouver home, where a friend of the girl who lived downstairs, stole her new computer right out of her kitchen, She, immediately moved out. She wasn't sure why someone would want to do something so injurious to her. It hadn't been so easy, to start from scratch again, in the first place. The computer was to be a tool for her, to get herself going with private students. Nevertheless, for whatever reason, this stranger decided to make her life miserable, thus she was on the move.

With fury inside, she stayed with her friend Tatiana, for a short-term arrangement. Then things just got stranger, and explosive, between the two strong women, as Tatiana had her boyfriend staying at the place, as well. She knew it was really none of her business, but this boyfriend was nothing short of a pariah. Things got much too close for comfort for Shirley, who couldn't but help to let her friend know that this man was a slime, for reasons, she had this feeling that he had not just one other woman on the side, but probably many.

It's an old cliché that had become a realization; that a man can come between the friendships of women. She dared to admit her mistakes, but her life was unraveling faster than she could keep up with, in many aspects. The interminable search for a place in Vancouver became more difficult as she was left to have to room with someone who had two large dogs in a small apartment. He made it a cross that he had to bear that he was also battling AIDS.

She had nothing against him, but was only to withstand this lifestyle, for a but a brief time. It was his kindness, that she was regretful about, and she hoped that he would continue to live well. She was undaunted about the disease.

In recent terms, the fight against AIDS had all but been won. At St. Paul's Hospital in Vancouver, there was a super drug that had been fashioned, that almost obliterated the disease. What really bothered Shirley was this man's treatment of his large dogs. After that experience, she vowed not to have a large dog. Dogs required an intricate set of commands, that would only come about, with strict adherence to training. She had been asked on more than one occasion, to take this gentleman's dogs for a walk, and at first did it, with enthusiasm.

The enthusiasm wore down right away, when on the occasion of going around the seawall, something she had always held dear, the dogs pulled her around with such force, that she had sore arms, and a sore back. Many people don't want to train their dogs, simply because, many people were lazy. If there was one thane to Shirley's existence, it was that there existed, a plethora of lazy people. The most annoying of this type of person, were the ones who were only lazy physically. These people possessed busy active minds, but were unable to get their bodies to follow through.

Not only, were they not able to move on these ideas, but they were always the people who were compelled to tell everyone around them, what they should do, to invoke action. She had tried very hard not to be hypocritical. Once in a while, everyone is a hypocrite, but it wasn't something that came naturally to her. She had learned from one of her sisters, that hypocrisy was something that some people were compulsive about. Shirley tried not to mirror that kind of behaviour.

Trying to follow through with most of her good ideas, and a lot of times, even her bad ideas, had become second nature, throughout her life. Perhaps there were times, that she should have given things more time, even when she knew, she was uncomfortable. Shirley's behaviour was marked by bailing at the earliest opportunity, when things got too weird for her. Her impetuous nature was sometimes to her detriment, however, this was her truth, not for anyone else, was it their truth.

Really, who are we, as individuals on this earth, to learn whatever we can from one another, to judge the actions of others. Even if the other people are ones that we love intimately, no one can have that perspective. She had remained soft inside, even with all those decades behind her. This life was meant to be full of highs, and lows. Shirley had become peaceful about the fact that, especially for those she loved deeply, there was agony in her soul, when things were not as they should be.

Her idealism got her into trouble, but there was no other way that she knew how to be. Those with such enormous imaginations, were the ones so susceptible. The cliché that the mind plays tricks on our consciousness rang true for her time, and again. It wasn't something that she grew out of with age, and experience.

With no other choices about where to live, Shirley ended up living with one of her acquaintances who she had met through the art scene under some strange stipulations. It was to be only a temporary arrangement, she was to sub-let a two bedroom apartment, while her friend lived in Mexico.

What a monumental task that turned out to be, given the context, of the situation. The return of her friend, under whose name the apartment was registered, was not known, because he was going to Mexico, to fight for Canadian citizenship status, with someone he had married, who had been deported by the Canadian authorities. Phew! Under this type of pressure, and with really not knowing how long she would live there, it was sad that, she saw this as the only alternative she had. The apartment was so well appointed, there was plenty of room. It was right on Nelson Street, only two blocks from where she had lived, for eight years.

She had no idea of the resistance that she would have to face, from the superintendent, who lived right on the premises. She was a miserable, nosy woman who really had nothing else to do, but to track the goings on of the people, who lived in the building. She had gone so far as to tell Shirley that she couldn't have certain guests there, either as renters, on a temporary basis, or just to have friends, over night. This was no favour that her friend was doing for her. She was being used, completely duped. Yet, through the whole year, she struggled getting people to live there, who didn't know, for what duration of time.

Her so called friend, had made it clear that her only job was to ensure, that she kept the place for him for whenever, he decided to return. She was so used to having people put conditions on things with her, that she would seem the natural choice to take this on, but her luck was thin. She had to contend with three different roommates, who disregarded who she was, as a person. These were people who had no courtesy to even want, to get to know, who she was. It was no wonder though, she had to rent the place for an undetermined amount of time.

The first roommate was only going to rent the extra room for a few months. She was fine with that, as she seemed to like this woman, who was a pianist, on a cruise ship, and just needed the place for a few months while dry-docked. At this point in time, Shirley was sure that she would only be at the apartment for a couple of months, anyway. This living arrangement turned into a farce, as this woman wanted Shirley to feel sorry for her, and to help her with the rent. Meanwhile she herself, was not in that position.

In fact, upon her arrival to Vancouver, she had walked around to the various language schools in town, proud to carry her new resume, and her certification for ESL. The first school she walked into, she was met by the director, who was only too assertive to tell her, that the certification she held in her hand, meant absolutely nothing, in Canada. She had been told right from the start that the school with which she studied, and with which, she devoted almost two years of her work to, was affiliated internationally, with all English institutions. She believed this phoney claim, without question.

Now here in a city, that is one of the most expensive cities to live in, the doors were shut to her. She couldn't teach English for any school, that would pay a decent wage. This fact was deeply disparaging to her. She did not know what she would do to recover. So not only did she have conflicts going on for her with gainful employment, at every turn, she also had to go up against trying to find people, who she could trust enough to live with her, amicably.

Shirley never had considered herself a difficult person to get along with. This was not her perception of herself. She had tried to consider every point of view. The mere fact that conflict during this time, was an inevitability, sent her over the deep end. Time went on, and her friend had not returned, and Shirley was still left with a two bedroom apartment for which, for some inane reason, she felt ultimately, responsible.

She just didn't know when to raise the white flag, and that perpetuated her friend's scam of her. The next roommate was someone Shirley could tell was full of the spirit of no nonsense. She could feel that this girl was hateful, of the type of person she was, and she felt choked, by her ominous presence. On the move in day she should have taken a clue, from the elaborate lock, she had installed on her door. What kind of person would have a roommate, who would install a lock? This wasn't the kind of living arrangement she had wanted. It wasn't that she wanted someone who was her other half, just someone, that could mildly trust her. As fate would have it, she had to force this person out. This did not happen easily. This woman had gone to the nosy superintendent, with a smear campaign knowing that the manager was very open to speculation, when it came to tenants.

She had learned too much about people through this year, but more was yet to occur. If this wasn't enough, the next roommate was apparently, a former addict. Yes, after one month of living with a young girl who claimed that she was moving out from a bad boyfriend experience, She was pulled into drama, which was way above her head. Whatever happened to the adage, that good things happen to good people? This parade of depraved souls was to continue. After having to worry about her roommates tricks, coming into the apartment, in the middle of the day, and doing who knows what, she had to get yet, another roommate. This one was at the eleventh hour, on rent day. He was a young Russian man, who presented himself as a hockey player, and had the devilish good looks, like Brad Pitt.

Yes, it does get better. At this point, Shirley didn't really care, as long as he paid his half of the rent. With insipid insinuations, and innuendos, she became only partially aware that this young man, wanted more from her. She was not, at this time ready to give anything, to anyone. She was completely spent. trying to keep this apartment for a friend, who had pinned her to a corner, to keep his place, the rent that was affordable, while he was down in Mexico, doing who knows, what. Whose life was Shirley living?

Her work had become pressurized as well. Being an English tutor wasn't enough, for some of these affluent students who had come to Canada, to buy their way, into citizenship. There were so many corrupt people, who were indoctrinated in their countries of origin, whereby, they could buy anything. Shirley found herself at their mercy, because of her cruddy, credentials. Teaching was something that she had become highly skilled at, so there was no denying her compulsion, to want to pursue any avenue, she could to make it work for her. Under duress, she had discovered that there was a black market for essays, at the university level. It started out so innocent, on her part. She was meeting with a dental hygiene student, who looked like anyone's mother from Iran, at the central library.

The two of them sat down, and with eyes movements, that could only be unnatural she was asked if she would write an essay, for this non-descriptive woman. Her response was of course no, but, from that time on, this sort of exchange, took on a life of its own. Before she knew it, she was churning out ghost writing essays on a regular basis, to make ends meet. There was one student who actually looked her right in the eye at the public library, took the essay from her hands, and walked away, without paying a dime.

Thus, in a brutal way, Shirley found herself imbibed inadvertently, into a life of crime. Her wise nephew Chris, made her feel better about it by saying, it's all just theory anyway. Whether or not that was true, beyond that justification, she wasn't the one submitting these, under false pretenses.

There appeared to be fever pitch going on in the air in Vancouver, at this time, as the city was preparing for the Olympic games. In consequence, there were a flood of foreigners on its streets. She felt this push, like no other time ever before. There were buildings coming up at remarkable speeds. Even in a relatively quiet area, like west of Denman Street, the fever had hit. Memories of jack hammers in the summer of 2009, right across the road, sent shivers down her spine. She had lived there for over eight years, so this was unprecedented, in her memory. She came in contact with so many different people, during that time period, and it was all so confusing. Finally, she had reached her breaking point, what with not knowing when her friend was going to reclaim his apartment, while being enraptured by this new young Russian boy, who had some kind of weird affinity to her. She was old enough to be his mother, this was way beyond reason.

At the very last minute, and as a very last resort, she jumped ship on the apartment, that was not even her own, to begin with. Having to manage the place was proving too much for her. Now in a fury, she walked out on the apartment, and was asked at the last minute by the Russian boy, to co-rent a house in Chilliwack. She didn't know anything about Chilliwack, except that it was cheap to rent a house there. So, like a person trying to escape persecution, she sped off on the highway, with a 26 year old Russian construction worker, supposed hockey player, to rent a house in Chilliwack. It seemed like a good idea at the time. What was this woman an adrenaline junkie? This wasn't a 20 year old woman, experimenting with things in her life, trying to find out what will work, and what will not work.

She was supposedly an older, more mature, form of herself. Within two minutes of arriving, she had known, it must have been desperation, that had led her here. Chilliwack was a ghost town; just there so that the corn farmers in the area could have a place to do their shopping. Sure, she had contended with the smell of the 16th century sewage system in Guadalajara, but that did not compare to the waft of fresh cow shit coming from the fields all around her, in Chilliwack. What the blazing was she doing there? As if the universe was hearing her call, she was thrown a few life lines, during her six months there.

First off, the Russian boy had to be eliminated from the picture. For some unknown reason he fancied that he could completely take advantage of her, in what ever way he wanted. Suddenly he appeared like a tramp, walking around the house in his underwear. Was he possessed by some Czars of his heritage, thinking that the way to Shirley's heart, was by flaunting himself to her? Shirley knew from experience that, indeed, though he had the young face, and good looks now, these were not to last, once he opened his mouth. He immediately began to talk to her, as if she were some subservient being, who would be nothing, were it not, for his presence. Really, how could someone go from zero to 360, in a blink of an eye? How arrogant was it, that this person could think that he had a hold on her? Besides, through his underwear, Shirley could see that his penis was the size of her baby finger. That must have been what sparked this young man's angst, after all.

On the occasion of driving into town, the two had engaged in a heated argument, and this boy was observed by people walking the streets as a threat. One such stranger who the Russian almost ran over, offered to fight him, with his fists. She did not owe this person any money, nor did she even owe him any explanations. She knew, that in order to take control of the situation, she would have to hatch a plan. It was operation get rid of the Russian time.

No one really knows what it must have been like to live in Russia, but this was Canada now, and why do we Canadians have to be embattled on our own turf? It wasn't natural for her to be in warrior mode, but this was the time. With gumption in tow, she had managed to make the acquaintance of a native Chilliwack man, through going to her next door neighbour's house party. The six foot four inch broad, chested Dustin was like a god send to her, at that time. He was but a fool himself, but he was able to show up at Shirley's door, and make enough of an impression on the

Russian, to scare the boy off.

The Russian packed his bags, and was gone; no longer a threat to her well-being. She had even had the chance to be witness to him putting the bags into the trunk of the cab. So with some relief, Shirley had to once more, fill a second room, in a shared accommodation.

The problem lay in Shirley's misjudgment of character. When first meeting people briefly, it is quite precarious to make that call of whether they are a stand up kind of person, or not. Another thing that she had in her disfavour, was that she definitely, immediately, needed a person to fill in the gap. She didn't have the time, or the money to play with. The rent had to be paid yesterday.

Shirley was dealing with people who were in desperate situations, not at all like her own. She was a good person who actually was faced with the fact every day, that she was born into abject poverty. This wasn't something that she had any control over. This was, so to speak, her lot in life. The next roommate was psychotic, and he actually flattened the tires on the riding lawnmower, that her landlord had provided for the property. It had seemed that, this unwitting woman could not, get a break. One roommate in Chilliwack, proved to be above board over all of them.

Fate at this time, smacked Shirley around right to the edge, and then someone, like an angel bringing light into her dark corner, would swoop in for the rescue. She garnered allies during this time, just enough to make it through those dark hours. One such life saver, at the time, was her one solid roommate, and another was her one solid student. The little boy was eight years old, and his father was there from Korea. She was paid well to teach him three hours of English lessons, per week. Just being there with him, in his room, surrounded by his favourite toys; she was light again. She was able to see the progress she had made, and in a show of respect, his father took her out at Christmas time, for a feast of sushi, like no other.

She had made other professional contacts in the six months, while she was there. There was also an epic research project that she had ongoing, with a PhD. Grad student, who needed her acute accuracy, to go through stacks of materials. When she fell, it seemed there was always someone to lift her up. Her work provided the esteem that was, as refreshing as, standing under a waterfall, letting the water caress her soul.

She had also made a true friend in Charla, who lived in the area, and was there especially when she needed her most. Two more roommates had to be eliminated during the time, one turned out to be someone boarding with the next door neighbour, who thought that it would be fine not to pay his rent, and the other was a mere teenager, who wanted her much older boyfriend, to live there as well.

Shirley finally had enough, the white flag was waved, and quite quickly, she packed up her things to basically, flee. Charla had arranged to help her get out of dodge.

With a sketchy at best, place to stay in Vancouver, Shirley landed once again. there in February 2010, just in time for the fabulous Winter Olympics. She had managed to get a job working for an English conversation school. This job turned out to be an outrageous scam. The proprietor claimed that she didn't have to pay Shirley, because the students didn't like the class. This was how this woman operated. The classes were fine, the students were engaged! As a teacher she knew the signs, when a class was failing. ESL students it seemed liked to get the teachers to give them a 'trail class' and they go around taking these free sessions in perpetuity. She was set up, that was guaranteed.

The owner had her secretary take part in the classes, and would make any excuse basically not to pay the employees. Bang, bang! Depleted, and on the move again, Shirley ended up living in a rundown, essentially, illegal boarding house above some shops, on East Hastings. This wasn't what life was supposed to be. The downward spiral had reached a point that one could not, nor did anyone have the energy, to recover from. She was ashamed, but at the end of the day, the only person she really needed to answer to, was herself.

The will to keep going, to keep trudging through the warped temporal shift that she was going through, was done. Ultimately, she felt that this was it, she was done. Then, like an angel of mercy, by chance, she ran into her niece Carly, who just happened to be stepping out of the A.T.M. area, on Hastings Street, and in one of Shirley's life defining moments.

For every question, there must be an answer. That very same evening, Carly was attending to her friend's place, to watch the gold medal hockey game. She was welcome there with open arms. The game gave everyone a reason to be happy, especially Shirley. By some strange, twist of fate, she was rescued, and from being in a world that had spit her out, more than a few times, she knew that she was loved. There was no more time though, that Shirley could just rest, and let the shadows swallow her up. She had to admit defeat, that Vancouver wasn't the place that she needed to be, at that time.

She called her faster-than-the-speed-of-sound brother George, and just like that, her one-way flight to London, Ontario, was booked for only one week into the future. George knew his sister, and the faster he could get her home, the better. She was in a tight dilemma this time, she had really done it, painted herself into a corner, that was for sure enough for her to go back into the ice, the sleet, the snow, and the hail. Being ashamed to the point that she was, by this time, she instructed George that she didn't want a welcoming party at the airport, or anything despite the fact that it had been seven years since she had even seen, her own mother.

Eleven: FASTER THAN THE SPEED OF LIGHT, OR SOUND

Words of Valor: World War I, was supposed to end it all.
World War II, showed them a way to end it all.
Wars right now, are big business.

It was with no fanfare then, that Shirley returned to her birth city. This wasn't a pleasant visit back to see her family; no it wasn't her vacation time. There would be no need for her to make a schedule to see who she could, in a small window of time. On the other hand, it was with relief that the occasion was not marked by someone's death, either. Her last time there was in 2003, to say goodbye to her sister Sheila.

It was March 2010, and there was an intangible force, that had brought her there again. She had found in the 19 years that she lived far away, that her siblings wouldn't act as they naturally would. That was to be completely understood. People are in a different mindset when they only have a short time to visit. This was all alien territory now. She hadn't been a strategist ever with her emotions, but truly, she wanted to be able to just fall into a puddle, and cry out all that was troubling her, inside. I t was never easy to be vulnerable, but in the presence of her family, she knew that it was impossible, for her to be that way. None of them acknowledged that for her. She was just to go around pretending that it didn't hurt, and taking the criticism, like it didn't matter. She forgave this in a way that was not superior, just she had hoped for something that was never to be. After all, that was what being a natural visionary was all about. There was a veneer around her to protect this extraordinary, impressionability. Her creativity was what had been the source of this void, there was a feeling of not belonging.

Shirley had no intention of making her family members a prisoner in her void. She didn't blame them for it, at all. They were there to be a reflection of who she was, and that was the gift that they all gave to her. She was extremely lucky to be from such a large family. Some of her siblings had to sacrifice parts of their individuality just to function. They didn't know better, had not the depth of perceptions that she had was exposed to.

Her eldest sibling, Barbara had helped her especially when she was becoming a teenager. But, Shirley by this time, had not come to consider this as home, her home was always Vancouver. It was her chosen home, this strange place, was just where she needed to be for an indeterminate lot of time. One person, who was for sure glad to see her back was her sister Tracey. T

racey had been through a divorce years before, and was in the newly single, empty nest phase of her life. Her birthday was just around two days after she landed, so just as the story went when Shirley was born, she was proud to announce to all her friends, that her little sister would be there, just in time to celebrate. Tracey recanted the story to her, about the day she was born, the final of the mob, of thirteen. Tracey skipped, sang, and told the whole neighbourhood, that she had a little sister. Now, they were able to be friends again. Shirley had hoped to be trusted to be close to her, again. Tracey had confided that through her maturing the relationships, within the sisters, were strained. She didn't trust them, she told her it was because they just didn't understand her. Tracey's rationale was that they just didn't want to know her.

Shirley had remembered the terrible fights, that her sisters had amongst each other, when their hormones were raging as teenagers. She would cower in the corner, at all of the screaming, and fighting. They would sometimes become so enraged with each other, that they would be physically violent. She knew as she matured, that these sibling rivalries were part of the human condition. There seemed to be an amplification of that, with four girls, all in the same proximity of age. It was taken to heart though for her, that to be competitive, was not where she wanted to see herself. It was ludicrous, to be racing against each other, for what end? Perhaps it was an offshoot of Darwinism. It could be anyone's guess.

When a group of more than three women live together, in a confined space, the fur is bound to fly. What then, at this point in their adult lives, did they need to hang on to? Wouldn't it be so freeing, to get all of the angst, from all of the years, on to the table, and then just let it go? Shirley was able to be on the outside looking in, and to her, the objective viewpoint, just made more sense. Trying to be the peacemaker of the family, wasn't an easy task, especially when the older women siblings, can't contemplate your credibility. These were complicated relationships, that was for certain. What she did know was that it began to feel, as if there were resentments, that she was there, all of a sudden. Perhaps she was breaking their natural rhythm. She wanted them to be aware that some things were hurtful, but she wasn't one to go looking for a conflict. It would be best to keep the status quo, that was much more relevant to her role here, now.

The undeniable joy for Shirley in being in London, again after so long, was that though she did not have the material things to give, what she did have now, was time. Her mother was in the twilight of her years. It was amazing that Rosemary was so active still, even after everything she had been through, with raising thirteen children. This was an inconceivable feat! What Rosemary possessed was a graceful reserve along side a wily, sense of humour.

Shirley was just one among many people who admired Rosemary. She had married at the age of 70, after being widowed when she was 48 years old. Shirley spent as much time as she was able to, going to the senior's complex, to take in all of the time that she knew she would be privileged to have, with her dear mother.

When people reach their octogenarian years, they can either wither, and feel that they have no purpose in life anymore, or they can be like Rosemary, and find whatever pleasures there are, and hold on to those. This was unprecedented for her to behold, that she would know someone that much older than her, in an intimate fashion. This was not the alienated person that she thought she had been. Rosemary had a way of making Shirley feel needed for just her reactions, simply just for her, being. She wanted to be as authentic around her mother as possible. She had felt that Rosemary needed to really know who she was. She had hoped that this would not be a burden, because there were times that she did not feel at her best, that was a given.

There was a sense of fun, and excitement, around Rosemary. Though alcoholism had ruined many a person in the family, there were inroads, and lessons, being mapped out, every day. It was endearing for her to witness the strength of loyalty that her oldest brother Tommy showed towards his mother. Tommy had almost lost his life to alcohol, and it was with each day, fifteen years after he finally put down that bottle, that he wanted to show everyone he could; what life could be, if they would only be thankful every day.

Tommy was a shiny example now for the family, and it was his tradition now, even though he worked five days a week; that on Saturday, he would go over to the senior's complex, and take his mother out for lunch, to any place she wanted to go. Shirley could not have expressed to him without becoming tearful how much she admired his strength. This time is the only time, we have so it's best to make the most of it. That is, and was, the message that she could see him live out, right in front of her eyes.

Shirley's family was crowded, but she had managed to be able to spend one on one time with her mother, and that was what really mattered, after all was said, and done.

The reinvention process was not easy for her. Her pride had taken quite a beating. Somehow she was under her own strain living there back in London again. There were external things about the culture of the city, that wore her down. London is known all over Canada, to be the city with the least friendly, of citizens. Shirley felt this cold shoulder every day when she ventured out on to the streets. There seemed to be some type of unspoken intrinsic bigotry; a stale state of being, that she knew she didn't want to pay any attention to. The simple things, like purchasing a good from a store made, one feel that they were intruding on the cashier by being there, at times. Strangers wouldn't even acknowledge your presence. A random smile was completely out of the question.

This was not the type of culture that Shirley was accustomed to at all, in Mexico, she was enveloped in warmth, and could feel the passion of the people. In Vancouver, while people weren't falling over you to make your day sunny, there was a reserved acknowledgment from strangers, and when it came to customer service, there was no better place to be.

Shirley stuck out in London for the way she smiled, the way she dressed, and just her assertive demeanor. She had lived in some staggeringly populated cities, so there was no wonder that she didn't feel at home in London. She felt that while she had some close ties with a few of her extended family, she received some cold vibes from others. Carly was there as well, so that was a good person for Shirley to be able to relate to. Carly knew how it felt to be an alien. Shirley also had Justice, her nephew there, who had lived in New York, and Paris. Her other most well traveled sister, Shannon lived there now as well. In fact, right during this epoch of time the whole family all lived in one town. That had not been the case in decades!

There were just some important elements in family relationships that she had wished could have been more functional. Again, she had to remember not to want something that was never going to be. Who was she really, to put forth expectations? Most people do the best that they can, and the others, well they just didn't have any significance, anyway. Why give credence to those who couldn't give a rat's ass about you anyway? She found sometimes that she had put a lot of heaviness on people, and places, that she perhaps, should not.

Her sense of freedom didn't fit in with London at all, but she didn't want to have to rein in who she had become, just to suit others. She wasn't there to offend, such as some artistic people tend to do. She put a lot of thought into how others would react. Shirley was calculating that way. This could get her into trouble sometimes. Those that hid behind their masks didn't like to be called out. Shirley wanted to do this though, she was willing to take her chances, but not in a grandiose way. To be polite was to be godly. Shirley wanted people to remember her for how she made them feel, but sometimes people need to know the truth. She didn't want the people in her closest relationships to think they could be superior, nor did she ever want them to be superficial, either.

She felt that with her family. there were rules of conduct, it was just that by her being the youngest, she was the one being told all of their rules. She didn't feel that she had her clear voice. While that was the truth, she did have to allow for the fact that many of them had not known her for nineteen years. So much can become distorted over time. She was competent enough though, she only knew what was true for her, and she wanted to know what other people considered the truth.

One of Shirley's most enduring family ties was with her brother Fitzgerald. Fitz had been like the watch tower for her all throughout her youngest years. For some reason, he had taken on the role as guardian to her. When at the very tender age her father died, Fitz had been one of his favourite sons. He was the one who Gideon would call upon to do all of the father son bonding special things with. Shirley remembered that Fitz was allowed to drive, when he was twelve years old.

One of her earliest memories with her brother was when, he had to go to orchestra practice on Saturday mornings, and he would take her with him. She was in awe of him, with his cello playing the music made by angels, and played by angels. This was her first introduction into the fine arts. Fitz was just a slight little boy of eleven years old, and the cello nearly covered up his entire body. His uniform was a starched white collared shirt, navy blue polyester dress pants, and a big navy blue, velvet, bow tie. At that moment, Shirley saw her rough, and tumble brother in a whole new context.

The delightful part of their early years was that Fitz was only too proud to introduce his little sister to all of his friends. He was brazen in his words about her to strangers. She would turn red, and hide her face from embarrassment. Fitz didn't see that having his little sister tag along on his excursion as an intrusion at all, in fact he relished it, but really he was assigned to be her babysitter on those excursions. She didn't mind, most of the time. The music made her heart sing, it was natural for her to enjoy it.

The musical appreciation aside, what she did mind was having to skate in the dead of winter outside for hours, in the freezing wind. Fitz wasn't an expert babysitter, he was but a boy himself, and liked rough housing play like boys do. Shirley's skates would be done up so tight that the circulation had gone out of her feet, and she wouldn't feel it until the end of the day, the feeling would start to come back into them, and she would feel would only can be described as excruciating, tingling pain. She would cry, and Fitz wouldn't know how to handle that.

The odds were definitely not in little Shirley's favour either, when it came to playing hockey with Fitz, George, and her brother, Vince. She learned from an early age how to assert herself. The act of crying very loud didn't seem to hold too much credibility with her young brothers. There were many times that they got a kick out of it. The boys didn't cry, they would just play fight. She observed that even if one of them got hurt they wouldn't dare let the others know. She would look back on those early days, and joke that she was raised by wolves. There did exist a dog like interplay amongst them, that would not be denied. She was one of the lucky ones in her family though, not having to have the heavy responsibilities at such a young age, as the older ones tended to. In her case, she remembered that she was able to play, just like all children.

Fitzgerald had a loyal streak in him, and he had matured into his most treasured of roles as father to his two sons. Shirley was able to spend many hours with them now. In the time that she had been away, Joel and Aaron, had grown into young men. Fitzgerald's wife Janet, was the rock of their family. She found that right from the start of this time, that she was accepted by Janet with open arms, and with a warmth of understanding that she could not be more abashed by. Janet had a reserved strength of character, but just below the surface, Shirley acknowledged her sensitivities. The two of them had a lot in common that way, only Shirley was much more impetuous, and was the veritable life of the party. There were only appropriate moments when Shirley could be reserved.

Fitz and George, played a big part in getting Shirley situated back in London. They would only go so far with her though, and then would let her go to see where she would land. From 2010 to 2011, she struggled to get her act together. When she did land employment, it wasn't a prestigious job at all. It was having to monitor primary school children both early in the morning before school, and then after school until 6:30, at night. This was a disaster position to be sure. There were no happy, smiling children looking up at her everyday. These were children who were angry, hungry, frustrated, and tired from being at school all day. Who could blame them?

She had to travel clear across London from the North end, to the West end, back and forth, two times per day. The schedule was brutal and there were no rewards in it, at all. The icing on the proverbial cake came when on a rainy blustery day in November, Shirley had to wear rain pants on her bike, and hung them up in the classroom. Behind her back in a sneaky move, one of the little girls, took a pair of scissors to them, and cut them in two. She was devastated. She had put so much of her energy into this job, and really tried for harmony with these children. With the threat of this type of incident occurring again, Shirley took her things for the program, and returned them to the office.

This was a long day for her in retrospect, and the pay didn't begin to cover her. Besides she knew that she would be laid off every summer. The good thing that came out of the position was that she had to find some sort of vehicle, besides a bicycle, to get there across the great distances, she had to travel everyday. Through going online, and doing research, she found the a most amazing solution. Shirley bought an electric scooter that looked like a little motorcycle, but did not run on gasoline. Everyday she would plug it in during her lunch hour, so that it could make the distance.

This was her freedom, as the public transit system was slower than walking. It stood out amongst the back drop of London in an amusing way. It was bright orange, and the front of it looked like a bumble bee with it's mirrors, and lights. She didn't care about how it looked, because to ride it, she felt like she was a kid again. For the typical narrow minds of London though, she was treated with disdain from the motorists, and from the London Police. In the two years that she rode the vehicle, the police in London pulled her over three times, for the most trivial of things.

Shirley knew that her brand of bold flexibility, was not welcome in that town. It only stung when on an occasion, that she had to get to work that the policeman told her to take it off the road, because it was missing a peddle. There was a ferocity in his tone of voice that made her feel, as she had always been made to feel growing up, there in the government projects.

There seemed to be an underlying disrespect for anyone that didn't have material wealth. She had crossed into both worlds there as a child when she had to carry her violin through the neighbourhood where most of the people lived on Welfare. There were times of humiliation, when she would have to go to school, without lunch. The kids she attended her special music school with all had the means to do all of the charity events, and hot lunch days. She was quiet about her disparity. It cut through her that here she was, a grown mature woman, and that now she had to flash back to those times when she could do nothing about it.

Twelve: THERE'S NO PLACE LIKE HOME

Words of Valor: Stunning beings only show like a flicker, never hang up on them.
The sugar of romantic love, is the most redeeming of it's qualities.
Love is such a huge concept, that there have to be many kinds.

Her living arrangements in London had become unbearable after the first year, that she found herself with neighbours who were drug dealers, at the large apartment complex, where she laid her stuff down at. She had found a good position finally, with a health care provider, so the time was ripe, to move into a more suitable accommodation. She had found an affordable place in the heart of Old South London, that was part of a four-plex, in a turn of the 20th century, mansion. The stair case was so steep leading up to the suite, that one could get a nose bleed. It contained a gas stove, and a claw foot tub. It was a small, but cheerfully appointed place, that included a washer, and dryer. She was thrilled with the location, so she eagerly made her move there.

There always seemed to be a catch, and this time, it was in the form of an 80 year old man, who didn't actually own the house, but was the main, caretaker of the property. At first, she just thought he was a friendly old soul, but as the weeks passed, he turned out to be an old man that made unwanted advances toward her. She was utterly shocked. She had never been in such an awkward position before. She had lived in so many different contexts, that she was sure that no one could shock her; but, this one took her for a loop.

Shirley had a way of trying to dial into people's brains, to discover how they think. In this case, of having to avoid the advances of an octogenarian, was beyond Shirley's innate, scope. I didn't matter, because no one would even believe it. So the place began to deteriorate, with Shirley having no use of her toilet, for three days. Another bad decision in the bin.

The next move, was three blocks up the street, so not such a hassle, after all. She had called on five of her young nephews to move her from this place. The staircase was treacherous, but in the blink of an eye, it was finished. The young boys had moved her in with little trouble. The next suite, in a house, in the same neighbourhood, was good, for the most part. she had a very clean, and well appointed place, with hardwood floors throughout. Alas, it was just not meant to be, that the last place she lived in London, was occupied by the home owner's young 20 year old son, and his psychotic girlfriend. This living arrangement had become intolerable. Shirley received the news that here, one good thing, her job, was laying her off permanently.

The rapid changes in Shirley's life, had made her feel unsteady for two years. It had never been her ultimate life dream to live out the rest of her life in London, Ontario. She could look back, and be reconciled that she had done her very best. It wasn't completely a love fest for Shirley. Being a citizen of British Columbia for just over nineteen years, had changed Shirley in many ways. The people of the coast of B.C., feel a strong relationship, with their land. It is incumbent on them to be diligent with the delicate landscapes.

All culture is partly based upon the environment. The priorities for Canadians are to meet the challenges of the evolution of the economy based society. The globalized world is unfolding in ways that are much more, bold than anyone, had ever imagined before.

Shirley was part of the technological revolutions of computers from their inception up until, the present time. She had become much more far-reaching in her ideologies. The rest of the world is struggling with the loss of natural resources. Canada is to take a strong hold of the management of natural resources. Her being had longed to hear the stories of the elders of B.C. Our ancestors had enough information to stop the infiltration of pollution, but the highly politicized misappropriation of wealth took on a life of its own. Right in front of her eyes she was seeing the destruction caused by the elite.

The culture of Ontario was driven by industry. The industrialized state, was therefore, the mainstay of everyday life. There was a different edge to Ontario people. Some of these sharp edges, were due to fundamental distrust. Shirley could not be let to give in to it. In an ideal world all of us humans could trust in each other. It was a resentful way of being. It was an indication of where her morals had moved forward. She did not want to endure more of it. She did not want to live with the nagging guilt it would cause her. It wasn't any one person's fault. Cultures are consistently changing, so if ever there was a time for things to change in London; Shirley had no doubt that they would. She just felt out of place.

Now when she would enter her home, if the girlfriend from downstairs was around, she would either run into the house, and slam the door, or forcibly turn the other direction. It was rude behaviour. Shirley had been all too familiar with feeling ostracized. She was at loose ends. It had turned out to be a catastrophe in a way. She wanted to be able to have more of a bond with her sisters. It wasn't to be, in however many years Shirley had lived, whatever she had accomplished, she just didn't feel that acceptance. The concept of sisterhood was not held to any sort of high priority.

She had felt what the woman team friendships had been, and wanted that with her sisters. She had grown to become a person with a sense of the importance, of trustworthy allies.

Circumstances had played a large role in Shirley's conscious perceptions. She didn't want to be sidestepped anymore. She was a woman with high moral oaths, a curious mind, and the need to be free. Being watched as if under a microscope, was not the way to go.

Life was full of a succession of failures, losses, and winnings.

Shirley missed the moist air, the gentle rain, the soaring trees, and the fire in her heart that she had left in Vancouver. It wouldn't be so easy to say goodbye to her dear mother who she had come to be so proud of.

Rosemary had chosen to live out her last years with the man she had married at the age of 70, in 1999. Nelson was like the bionic man, having battled out many health issues, in the time that Shirley had come to know him. Rosemary would confide in her daughter how afraid of Alzheimer's disease she was; that she was now living through on her own, with very little medical help.

Love was about compromise in the large schematic. The union of two people must join together their souls. Shirley admired her mother's bravery. Rosemary was determined to hold on, and take care of him. Her mother had taken an oath, and had lived that oath. Hers' was the generation that had to live through devastatingly-disastrous social upheavals. Shirley couldn't have imagined what it must have been like to send your brother off to the war, and your boyfriend, as was the case of her mother. The streets would become desolate. Many families were faced with a great loss in a loved one. There would be no men around town.

The children would have to grow up very quickly, out of the age of innocence. Rosemary had been the only daughter of a miner from Northern Ontario in Timmins. She was truly treasured by her mother, and father. Theirs was one of the families that did not suffer during the Great Depression. The pain was severe for Shirley's mother, when her parents ultimately divorced.

Children are shattered by divorce. What little they do know about the world suddenly changes over night.

Rosemary had certainly known loss in her life. Both of her parents died in their early 50s. He brother had died in his early 50s, in the same year when she lost her husband, at the age of 54. For so many years, her life had been engulfed in sadness. Shirley felt that she wanted to know Rosemary more. Two years in the same city was the opportunity to strengthen knowledge, and narrow the gap. There is only one chance to make things right, and timing was everything. She had felt that time had been on her side.

It made her nervous to think that the door would be closed had she not opened it. Going to London had been in a way an escape from the shame that Shirley had felt with her life in Vancouver. She had to keep that in mind then, for her next move. It was wrong to have to feel not good enough. An absence of a plan had not worked for her. Her next move had to have some type of higher purpose. After all, her mother had reminded her that she was getting a bit long in the tooth for such big moves. Shirley had been dismissive of that comment. Rosemary had candidly proclaimed that she didn't want her to leave. It was as though she may have an emotional outburst.

She did not want to disappoint her mother. It had seemed that she did that so often. There was still some hurt places there. Those are the places that one must establish not to visit too often. Self-pity is not a good state of affairs, by any estimation. Shirley wanted to be regarded with pride. It was so damaging to be up against scrutiny. If the world were that intolerant than there wouldn't be as many people as there are. That was the real crisis. There is a population explosion phenomenon going on. Shirley had been the result of some chain of events.

She had felt that there was nothing that would threaten the times that she shared with her brother Fitzgerald, and his family. Her brother had made her proud with the way that he treated his wife, and his children. Fitz, could fill a room all by himself. His sons were a complete hybrid of both his brother, and his wife, Janet. There were so many times that Shirley had felt compelled to visit the couple at their home. She had been able to follow her brothers around at their place of work. There had to be a time that she would go back to Vancouver, sort of a foregone conclusion really.

This time would be different because, she wouldn't go to Vancouver, but she would go to the island. After loads of research, she ended up choosing the port city of Nanaimo, as her new home. This time she wouldn't be alone, she would quickly come to know some people, and she would have a job. The best arrangement this time was for the place. She had secured her own cabin. That was what she had manifested in her imagination. She wanted to be close to the ocean. Vancouver was so close.

Shirley had been to Victoria. It was so far from Vancouver, to get to Victoria. She had tried to do the trip in one day. After two times of doing so, she had sworn that the next trip would be over night. The ocean air made a person feel so sleepy. The level of exhaustion after being on open water, was as if one were jet-lagged. The central island was seeing more industry, and Shirley was surprised by how affordable it was to live. It was the close proximity to the mainland, that really made the decision, an easy one.

The flight was booked the brave new step was to be made. Now at 44, Shirley was stepping on the plane to move across the country. That would be a total of three times. The other times that Shirley had moved were out of country. That was a total of two times. She was a roadrunner in the core of the word. It was time to set sights on the long range future. The past generations had ignored the long range. What was it that Shirley could do to launch herself into the present? There were fads that had lasted for centuries. She wanted to reinvent some enduring fad.

The access to knowledge is attainable anywhere, at anytime. Some cosmic shift of consciousness. The anarchy of the politics of the future have to remain visible. The world is ready to move in the right direction. The environment is the last to survive. Shirley had seen the water problem in Mexico. The whole population of the world is at risk of losing potable water. Canada has to hang on to that resource.

It was through an understanding of provincial politics that, she was further ingrained in the culture of the coast. The lines of communication between the public, and the government are very clear. She was amazed at the relentlessly loud activist groups, who represented special interests. It was a much, more polite way of living in groups. It has been proven that societies where much more discourse is going on, are intrinsically more democratic.

Shirley had an appreciation for the role of the diplomat. The Canadians must remain engaged in order to stand on guard for their freedoms. She had come to believe that much more could be achieved through a common ground. The visionaries of the 60s, and the 70s, were needed. In the time of her birth, she felt the vibe of the flower child. Through knowledge, belief, strength, hope, and love; she wanted to be part of the world. She had envisioned that her legacy would be her multi-faceted view of the document of our lives.

People need to feel that their values are expressed. She would be obliged to fill that void, and make it worthy. Life could not be examined under a microscope. That was for sure. Since everything is just energy, then every person, who we interact with everyday, will also be a product, in some minor way, of our energy. It was beyond any doubt that the brain could do things, that man could even ponder. There has to be some sort of code, that could unlock the secrets of life.

People were unaware of directions. She wanted to be part of it, as it was like one big celebration. The power of the mind can be used for constructive things. If we had the level of intelligence, we may be able to affect the communications, that we have with our brains. For Shirley, she knew that there had to be some information missing. There would be things imprinted on one's brain that will be indelible. Was there any possibility that all things that we experience as humans never leave us, in some corner of our minds?

One must observe and be sensitive to memories. She had some from as early as when she was just four years old. Most of the things that Shirley could recall, were traumatic experiences. The good experiences of her childhood, were the ones that she wanted to remember the most. If she could remember her own life formula, it was that, we are all the product of a series of events. A mob mentality dimension was inherent in Shirley's large family. They represented a strata of the human experience to be completely honest.

The sounds of the ocean, and the smell of the salt air were just what she had needed to do in this, one of her many, incarnations. This time around she had lowered her expectations to being accepted by society. How could one waste their energies upon the incessant discourse of our ever changing society?

Shirley had an affinity for Canada, in her appreciation for the culture of the region. No one need wear a label. The best measurement of success is a self-awareness. She was lucky to be a child of the 60s, and 70s, where social tolerance, were the orders of the day. She had even remembered being part of some grade school experiment. When she was in grade one, there were no walls between the classrooms of grade ones, to grade fours. They called it, the open pod system. Shirley was in grade one, and the one room school house, was full to the rafters. The floors were carpeted. She remembered the bright blue carpet, especially on the day that her grade one teacher forbade one of her classmates to use the bathroom, and the little girl couldn't hold it any longer, and peed right there, in front of approximately 40 kids, of all different ages.

She had learned about some harsh realities, such as public humiliation, from very early in her life. She was like a bank. It was time to give a piece of her to the world. The exuberance of youth should not be for violence. The fears for the future had to do with the rise of gun violence. No one wants to be subservient. There is a need to honour femininity, and get rid of mistrust. All women should be proud of themselves, and try to achieve their hearts desire.

Inevitably, with change there is pain. Everyone had the ability to be helpful, and polite. She was starting to get the bigger picture. At a point in our existence, that we have spent our youth, then comes a time when age does, take over. The image of father time, how he is some decrepit soul, with no hope. She didn't want this her mid-forties to be a time when self scorn would continue to be a theme. She had played all of those tapes in her memory bank at times, when she could not have gone so low. At the end of it all, who do we really have to blame?

Statements to ourselves should be an indulgence. One must come to recognize at which point something becomes self-indulgent. She had those moments. Those were the worst things for her to remember. She had always considered that she was the type of person who could present well toward others.

Shirley had no notions of becoming known, as an insufferable temper. Sometimes as she matured, she would find her tone as malicious. That could be a scary thing to be. One should want to be considered as rational, and kind. She had understood the entire human bondage dilemma.

Humans inherently resist social change. The thoughts that would go through Shirley's mind, when she would think about how she had been chastised for being a woman. She did not identify with the angry feminists prevalent of her time. To be truly representative of being a woman, one would show that change come about without force, or violence. Did people need protection, against themselves? That was what had taken over for people, it was their imaginations.

She had a glorified respect for artists. She knew when she was in the presence of some great ones. An artist could feel the pulse of people. Shirley could feel the tinge, when something had moved her core. An utter removal from the aesthetic is not tolerable in her world. She was prime to breathe into her role. The artist can exalt in failure. Frames of reference are always there. The sorrows of letting go from the attitudes, that make people weak, are not to be accepted.

A certain arrogance arose in Shirley when she was faced with having to be somehow responsible, for the sad indulgences of others. A woman can only be strong for the things that she values. Although reciprocity should be the norm, she wasn't sold on the idea. People should not have to rely on each other to fulfill every need. Shirley had seen people who were lonely, and had experienced her own loneliness.

Feelings are fleeting, more interchangeable, whereas, emotions presented, as more complex. There were things that would trigger bouts with loneliness. She had sensed that it came from acceptance from society. The women who is married is still considered more desirable, in society, than the single woman. Being single wasn't a shroud that Shirley wore around her. She had not identified as being one of a group of single women. There was the whole ordeal of owning property. The married couple are a much more desirable to give mortgage loans to. She had no collateral, and no financial fortitude. She had witnessed that for some people their relationship with money was on solid ground. There were actually people out there who didn't suffer under the pressures of poverty. Canadians don't have any grasp on what poverty is.

Shirley had been able to come to grips with the reality of the world. What she had been exposed to living in conditions of poverty in Canada, was nothing in comparison to what it must be like for people, in most any other country, in the world. She had learned that in many countries, there was no possibility of improving one's lot in life. We can only be witness to so many disasters in life before the pendulum swings in the other direction.

Thirteen: NOT MY FIRST RODEO, AND NOT MY LAST

Words of Valor: Life is an endless parade of spontaneous moments.
Waves of brilliance mark most of every day.
Be selective about what you objectify.

Admittedly, Shirley was very aware that there was always room for improvement, for every individual. How distracted must be the person who can tell others what they should do. She had never handled unsolicited advice so well. Some of the ever changing characteristics that she had was to crave, anyone who would take the time, to listen. She had found that there were so many people who didn't know how to listen. They couldn't reconcile any actions.

The only true vice, was one that you could never live without. Shirley had tried to conquer her demons. It was strange to be put up against others. This life was one great big exchange. When one had become so attached to people, they seemed to disappear. Their loyalties were part of the illusions that she had fed her mind with, in order to survive in a world, where she was unwanted.

No one was there to comfort her mind, sometimes in the darkest corners. The gravity of situations get lifted as time passes. Shirley did not find that things of the past were forgotten. The edges around the sources of restraint, had been dulled. People have all kinds of fancy notions. Acceptance is only reached at, through some more, series of events. She could see a break in the clouds, and her insides began to get all fuzzy, and warm. It was so much less a burden to have enough faith in fate.

When her life had spun in all sorts of directions, fate had intervened to bring her back down to earth. She wanted to form alliances with people, who were on their paths toward optimizing their well beings. The time was ripe, things would only just be a matter of hard, dedicated energy.

Shirley had known at what time to gauge her resistance to shake ups. The things in life that happen, and then afterward you remembered something as mundane, as brushing your teeth. It had to be amazing how the mechanics of the wiring of the brain, functions. One could not think of anything more attractive. The brain had to work just like a muscle. The unconscious skills had to be the most important ones, certainly the most hard working. The brain dedicates many hours per day toward the unconscious. How could that dedication go unrewarded was the mystery.

Intellectual people wanted to figure you out. She wanted to be in the company of fellow intellectuals. Society should recognize the ones who give their viewpoints. There exists a window to the soul of the artist, and the intellectual. There was no reason to be put in amongst souls that did not know their potential. She was tired of being dragged down by those who envied her. It played itself out like a threatened animal. Others are threatened by their fears of living in truth. Shirley found that many people put up guard rails around them, so that they are cemented to the fabric of reality.

She surmised that reality was a subjective experience. It differed for all. That could be seen in the way that people deal with crises, and their emotions. If there was one advantage to having that soft touch, was that all emotions are acknowledged. The suppression of true emotions, even negative ones turn into something else, destructive.

Shirley wasn't one to blast out her emotions over a loud speaker, neither did she suppress them at all. When issues surfaced, her reaction would be first in the form of frustration. Anger was a form of cancer. Shirley had seen people die of anger. She deemed that people who were angry really weren't cool. It was embarrassing to think about the things that people say in the fit of anger. Blame was the name of the game for angry people. There are things that people can do with their lives, that can avoid anger altogether. This emotion was the biggest waste of time of all emotions. There was absolutely no need to be helpless. Once in a while there would be some ritual that she would allow herself, where she could feel, that her soul was cleansed. Nothing from the outside, can take over. The romance of living was long overdue.

As if waking from a fitful dream, there Shirley was, trying to make her life over from scratch. What were the remnants that were worth keeping? There was a day in Chilliwack, when Shirley was walking down the street to her gym, when she saw in the sky, two rainbows. Not just one, but two, in a spectacular show of good things to come. The omen was lucky, she would have to be reminded of that day. It was a significant in that it seemed to send the message, not to give in. She had so far, been literally removed from situations. She did not want to go through her life, having to seek out the proper situations.

These life experiences that make us happy should be a natural occurrence. Perhaps she had just been all too diligent. She should learn to let go of the pain and disappointments. To contemplate these concepts are one thing, but to live by them, are another. She had proven the existence of God. He was, because we had merely conceived of him. Shirley wondered if he was a man. It could be that God is an alien. She had taken part in some of the discourse of her time about life on other planets. The discourse was not that unbelievable. She could conceive of aliens from another planet, quiet reasonably.

Her rationale was stifled when it came to the concept of God, as she grew up knowing it to be. Our levels of technology have allowed us to shed a light on many things, but aliens, and God, seem to always, get left out. There was a struggle that was silent. People were hesitant in Canada to shift their moral ideals. As anthropologists will attest to, people need to go through centuries, before they will shift their consciousness.

This is the great frontier that people hold in the highest regard. There were an army of protectionists out there in their own silent revolution. The fear would be of the uncertainty of life, and how we would carry on. Her ideals steered toward those in power, being the ones who were the most protective of people's potentials.

There were no predictors of behaviour, set in stone. The psychologists couldn't agree with each other. One could see clearly though, that people were guilty of being imprisoned. The temptations with power, and greed were obvious imprisonments. The legalities of marriage laid many people in ruin, they had no idea what they were getting themselves into. She had seen people cry from the depths of despair over a divorce. She was glad to be saved from that misery, and disappointment. Someone really crazy thought up that concept, divorce. Marriage had slowly become somewhat, obsolete, in her world. Women used to marry out of social position, they had absolutely no choice. She didn't see that sort of arrangement, as being beneficial in her case. She didn't possess a dowry.

A ceaseless curiosity was a vital element in Shirley's personality. This was what would transform her, so that she looked younger. She was to embark upon a life marker, where she wasn't afraid to test the waters. Shirley had gone through all of that, she was well beyond a debutante.

She had the cushion of all the years behind her. There was no basic need, to be accepted. What would cause the rise of this in her? Perhaps it was that she now felt the warmth of her surroundings, give her strength. There were mountains, rivers, ocean, and forests, right at the end of her street. What had made her so privileged that she would be able to reinvent time, and time again? She just had to get it right, so to speak. With the urgency of the situation at a standstill, she felt that she could accomplish notoriety, for posterity sake. The only need now, was the time, and place to set this dream alight. Nothing need be held on to from the past that didn't contribute in a positive way. She didn't want to shelter people from the things that she could realize.

She had every right, and had earned her spot there. Misgivings were just an excuse. She wanted to radiate openness. She wasn't a sheep and didn't want people to follow her like one. Shirley wanted people to be organically drawn toward what she had to say. There is a narrative for everyone. This is an individual, who has a voice that says things, that other people can relate to. She had no preconceived notions about it. All that her mind was focused on, was to put in the time, to finish the work. It didn't matter the time that was put in, just that there was representation. How she would regret it, if she didn't put forth her life.

She was put into a remarkable position, as a matter of fate. It was attainable through existence. It was that simple. Having set up her life, to rebuild once more, Shirley thought that she had hit on the right note.

If all we are as humans, are vibrations, then this felt like vibrating at a higher level. This could be a community of gardeners. The viewpoint into Vancouver, was spectacular. she could see all of her most vivid places she had been, in miniature form. Vancouver looked like a doll play set, or model. Shirley could see all of her places, as if they were on some magical doll, play ground. Floating there was easy. She had only traveled there when the weather was good for smooth sailing. She could come and go to Vancouver, any time at all.

It was but for a brief moment, when her welcome entourage had driven through the downtown core. Shirley's hood. It was fireworks time, and the place looked like an excavation sight of some kind. Her city was flying high in the sun, welcoming whoever wanted to have interesting things to see, as an onlooker. That was what set Vancouver, apart from every other city, there were always things for the eye to look at. It was a city teeming with a life style, that demanded health. It wasn't a city where one had to have a car. In fact, Vancouver was meant to be walked around in. There were nestled neighbourhoods, that didn't run for so many blocks.

Everyone was sort of on top of one another. If a person spent a lot of time in downtown Vancouver, they begin to find it growing smaller. Shirley was visible, when she lived there. Her little Denman Street cove, became the one street that provided everything she needed. It was difficult to go on that street, not done up. There was always the possibility of running into an ex-lover. Any single person living downtown Vancouver, should choose wisely when engaging in casual sex. The option is not there to be anonymous.

She saw the gay scene there as very easy to deal with. It made the core feel safe. There were some seedy sides to the gay life, but that was like any strata, in society. Where once Davie Street, was known for its hookers, it now has become full of community gardens, patio side restaurants, grocery stores, and good old liquor stores. In some areas, building codes have been set in stone, that provided enough low rise buildings, to keep the park lands. Shirley adored living downtown Vancouver.

Living on central Vancouver Island, was a welcome retreat from the chaos of living on the mainland. Nanaimo had originated during the push for coal. It had maintained its autonomy from urban spread, along it's core. This is due to the drama of the slopes of some smaller mountains, the way that the coastline is a dominant, yet winding, feature.

The setting was unparalleled for Shirley the Adventured. She had the occasion to visit Victoria more than a few times, but had not stayed in Nanaimo, but just once before. Again, like every time before, she was willing to take her chances. This time she liked her odds. What had been such a sore spot with her in London, was now completely cured here. Nanaimo had no shortage of friendly people. Shirley had found that she could easily manage her life here on the island. It was so much easier, when one could feel welcomed into the new culture. She was a welcomed addition. She was now in a comfortable mode, where people know that she's 'out there', but don't care one way, or the other. She hadn't heard any feedback that the opinions of the locals were, that she must be off her rocker, to be here.

Sometimes, she had experienced that underlying doom in her situation. It was sort of like that when she had first moved to Mexico. Shirley wasn't there to be on vacation. She was therefore rendered off her rocker right from the start. Not in this instance at all, with new introductions, she would explain that she had lived in Vancouver for many years, and the people here, would just know exactly where she is coming from.

There was no night life that she wanted any part of here. She was determined to have a life style that could afford her things that would reflect the years that she had put into developing her life portfolio. It was an opportune time to take hold of one's life, and turn things in a serious direction, for the long term. When one can think about something, one can do it. She had been using that technique very often in the past two years. She used her imagination as a very strong tool. She had been very interested in quantum physics, now it was time to put that interest into practice.

When it comes to the process of learning, throughout Shirley's experiences, she had come to a time in her life, to put the learning into use. Her mind worked in a way that she had to see the concept on paper, then absorb it, organically. Shirley had found it easier to attempt to absorb a concept by using her IPad. Technology is meant to be there to serve a higher purpose. She had truly believed that the way technology is perceived by the one using it, makes all the difference. Working with technology is a spiritual experience. The outcome is much more advantageous for her, when she can see visual pictures of what that concept represents. Machines can only make things better.

Mankind just didn't want to embrace technology, the way that it should be embraced. When Shirley really thought about it, there were technologies being used, through the eyes of the capitalist. She was aware that the marketplace was flooded with technologies, that were only meant to last a year. The main problem with a capitalist is, that they think that the world is one bottomless pit, that they can pollute until there's nothing left.

Advances in technologies are being fed to the public via capitalist interests. Those are the types of interests that nothing is seen very clearly through. She had been careful to choose things that she needed in her choice of technologies. Everything served a purpose, and those had the good intentions behind them. One could get involved with something lucrative, but that caused absolutely nothing, positive. She could see that people were boundless in their energy over the pursuit of nothing. It was time to bring that notion back, that caring was much more satisfying, than the pursuit of bargaining power.

She had seen people with money out on a shopping spree. The

cart is not big enough, so they use two. Forget being mobile, when you have so much stuff you can't remember what you have. People hid behind their stuff. Most people in our modern society, every day are engaging in some activity, that takes them away from reality.

Shirley was alright with the fact that living is a painful experience. Some people just don't want to fight it. They carry on with risky behaviours, in defiance. She could see that the world was like that. There were many levels to what is actually going on, at any given time. Virtual reality was a great thing. Everyone could try something out on screen, before actually doing it.

Having absorbed that into another context, what really scared her, were violent video games. The Canadian news had been noticeably flooded with stories about gun violence. She was worried about the future. Making good with the past, can make one very tuned in to the future. Shirley had opened the door, to the now. There were so many things one could do with time. She was beginning to get her footing once again.

Going as far-reaching as one could get is meant for few people. She was eager to be a life long club member. She would take her mind through things visually, and on paper every day. Who can you relate to, more than yourself. There were times when the self behaves in strange ways, so that one is not fully, in agreement.

To hear about a person who is battling their demons, brings to mind that they are just making the wrong decisions. Shirley was anxious to hold on, and not take on, being powerless. There were many things worth standing up to, and fighting for. She wanted that people were willing to make sacrifices for one another. The world was not being pulled around by egos and actually thriving.

She was in awe of people who could push all of that inside. They were the ones doing less talking. To this point in her life she had decided to remain brave. It was much better to see people at face value. She didn't like sorting through innuendos. That seemed like a waste of time, to have to read people's signals. It was good to have the knowledge though, to choose whether to know, some people. She had found that the niceties flew out the window, given a change of context. She didn't care what people thought behind her back.

All one ever has control over is, how they react to this knowledge, however unseemly. Sometimes we have to make adjustments. In many cases, one is obliged to walk the other way. Her level of maturity had shown it self, in trying to negotiate, the moment. ones didn't feel that it was right to drag people through your shit. There were some things about her, that people didn't need to know. She had been asked several questions through the years, and by now was aware of the spirit of the inquiry. Were people on the receiving end, genuine? It wasn't so difficult to tell these days. Some of us just give it away. People have a part of us that they can give away as ammunition. One must refuse to think at that level. What was the point of giving in? The mind does indeed play tricks.

The answer to the questions can be found usually in the moment. Shirley was full of speculation, but more often than not, her speculations had turned out, to be false. This was a lie proof world that we live in. She could see it in science. The more she had contact with doctors, the more that she could see that they do know what's ailing people inside. The body will reflect the diseases of the mind.

There really was only one way to orient oneself. If ever one had any hope at lasting through devastation, was to trust the instinctual mind. One must want to open up to listening intently to instincts. These are the pangs that happen in our bodies that go beyond words. Shirley remembered how that felt, with any man she had an attraction to. It was some gravitational pull that indicated fear.

Our bodies were meant to have those mechanisms built in, for protection. This is the fundamental root of survival. Life really came down to a game of survival. When a person is questioning everything around them, they are not truly living. She saw living as a tactile experience to be certain. There were endless thoughts that could come, and go.

Being a virgin was like living on the side lines. Shirley had been so relieved to lose her virginity. She had schemed in her mind how it was going to happen, months in advance. As the time had drawn near, she was actually in a panic, to get it over with. It did happen quite naturally, just after she turned 19, on New Years Eve 1987, with the captain of the football team, at her high school. This was a guy Shirley had admired from a distance, ever since she was in grade nine. Four years later, she had no way of knowing that her imagination, could make things come true.

Dreams are our imaginations, presenting to us the best of what we can live, in our reality. At such a young age, she was able to use some of those magical quantum physics, in her life. The problem is that the universe can be unpredictable as to the exact time line of events coming true. Shirley was willing to adjust to the unpredictability. There was always an inconsistent push, and pull in place. The details didn't make much of a difference, compared to the end results.

Life had taken on a resolute air, at the age of 45. Shirley was curious about people's motivations. She knew what drove her was that she wanted to bring as much comfort, and stability in her life, as she could. She wanted to draw together people, who were also racing toward goals. Life was a race. Shirley could see that she needed to do some things, that were in line, with who she was. There are those among us who never strive for the chance to live as an expression of who we are. She was at peace with the fact that, she didn't find her perfect man. For some of us, that doesn't last, when we do find it. Humans have to tap into what will truly optimize their talents, and aspirations. She knew she had all that she needed, to do something with her talents.

This was salmon country, here in, Nanaimo. It took some time to discover the river running through the back of the property that she lived on. The north end of the town, was where Shirley could see the suburban sprawl. She had liked the decidedly, old charm that the downtown area had. She could see the local news broadcaster from his big picture window on the main street, working strenuously on his laptop. Coffee was one of Shirley's favourite pursuits. The streets in the centre of town were dotted by commercial, and local coffee shops. Shoes had become important. She had to navigate the dramatic slopes thus far, on a bicycle. She was yearning for her electric Gio bike. Her weaknesses were not so highlighted here. The ocean front provided the vistas where one could feel the expansiveness of feelings.

What we say, and what we do should be synonymous. How did a person become bored? The options unfold, from our intelligences. We must not deprive our soul's direction. In this way then all aspects of what constitutes our beings, must be thoroughly considered. Humans are multidimensional beings. It started in Lake Titicaca, Bolivia and continued to passionately resonate. She could attest to that with remembrances of her visit to Machu Picchu, where her inner, outer, and a dimension above all others, were revealed. A visit there was an education in itself. This whole concept of things unfolding in an organic manner was born.

Those were the experiences that made a standout statement that were manifested attestations to your life. This was the lesson that was unfolding for her, in Nanaimo. The inner struggles or demons, persist when we deprive ourselves of being fully realized as human beings. That was a matter of awareness. Shirley was tapping into her sub-conscious self, in order to save her conscious self.

Humans are fusion. We are on a dimensional plane of existence, that does damage to our inorganic matter. One must strive to maintain the relationships, between these two entities. One could certainly not exist without the other. For this woman, the building of strong relationships with her past was a necessity. The two years spent back in London had been productive on some very subtle levels. Shirley was able to blend together the parts of her self that had been missing. Reminders from some other dimensions were what brought her back to this plane of existence that had eventually led to her being here, in Nanaimo. She was beginning to finally make sense of her role in all of this movement. It really started to make absolute sense. Besides, there were bunnies all over this place.

'There are no coincidences.' Let's make the best of our time here on this shabby plane of ours, in existence. She liked the word coexist. She wondered why so many times that people just wanted to fight with each other. What were they battling over? Shirley had never enjoyed being in someone's company, who always had fight words to say. She didn't want to be in opposition, with anyone.

No one needs to get the most credit for their deeds. She was embarrassed by those who wanted to be the centre of attention. For her it seemed that people shouldn't have to fight for attention. That would just come with having a community outlook. Shirley could see that in Nanaimo, that it was in their culture, that they want you to be friendly. People don't have to be your best friend, but she found that people engaged with each other in a community building way. To Shirley it was conveyed as a genuine acknowledgment.

There was no need to be in your face here on, Vancouver Island. This just wasn't a small town isolated by small town values though, and there is an active communication with, Vancouver. Nanaimo, wasn't a spectacular destination place, but it did offer access to all points on the island. She had felt much more isolated in Victoria. Victoria notably benefited from being the Province's capital city, but it was a far stretch from, Vancouver. Nanaimo, had flights that went to Vancouver every day, and at affordable rates. Shirley couldn't wait to see her doll, play house Vancouver model, from a plane. All things considered, it was a nice place to be.

The cabin was the size of a garage, but it had that country feel. Salmon habitat ran the back of the property. The cabin was not in the centre of town, but it was not far away. She was becoming familiar with the dramatic slopes of the streets. Things could move at a slower pace. There are many things to take into account from the environment. She was very sensitive to her surroundings. This was as serene a setting, as there could be, without the isolation factor.

The butterfly analogy had a reason for it's staying power. We are in the cocoon phase for a long time, where we wrestle around with these different versions, of our lives. We emerge from all of this nonsense, free from harm, and then we fly away into eternity.

The only thing wrong with that story is that we haven't reached that eternity stage yet, and many of us are afraid of what it may be. So far all us, as a group, have come up with some pretty freaky stuff. Shirley would have to agree that there are some things out there that are wrong. When your neighbours are salmons, you know that everything is right.

Friendships are bullet proof. She wanted to believe that she had made some good friends in her life. She had hoped that she had figured out how to be friends with some of her siblings. It was of great priority. No one was getting any younger. Many losses can be turned into gains. Not all losses, but many.

A journey through the parts of your mind that can learn about concepts like eternity are essential. These do not have to have a negative frame of reference at all. Shirley needed to open her mind to such possibilities.

Whatever is wrong can be fixed. The solutions present themselves naturally. People need to literally let the lead out. All of those things that are weighing us down. She could not see this, but through some sort of isolation. She was not intrinsically expressing this anymore. Shirley had conducted her life through a vacuum sometimes. This was inevitable to the evolutionary process. In order to stay focused on who she was, she had to go through periods of isolation. She could, in this way, gauge the measure of how it made her feel. To completely withdraw, would be like giving up. One didn't see that she had given up, but perhaps that was exactly what she was doing. We tend to build our own drama. How else could we survive if we are not reliving some element of drama? That's what Shirley used to keep her on her toes, when she needed to be.

It was a regressive tactic. Many times in life people feed their regressions. They should never move into the sphere of taking over your entire life. The addictive behaviours would come, and go for Shirley. She was grateful to have that impulse at bay. Addictions were so easily attained. She was aware that there were people, who could feel that impulse, with much greater veracity, than others. Just like everything, all of us are different.

Transcending the inevitable was an absurd notion. Shirley could hold her own values up, and revise when needed. It was a hallmark of all great people, that they are the ones who know their own weaknesses. She wasn't above weakness. We can choose to let impulsive behaviours take hold of us. That is when many people check out of the norm, and take a look at the abyss. Shirley was sold on the theories surrounding U.F.O.s. The technology has to exist.

The conspiracy theorists had chosen 2012, to be the year that a new world order be put into place. The Mayans, and the Incas, had ended their calendars for that year. Now here Shirley was, amongst all this hype, back in the part of the world where the environment sets the stage for discourse. The public had open discourse here on Vancouver Island. She recognized the broadcaster from growing up in London. He was a local personality in London, before he ever became one, here. There she was on the precipice of the end of days. Now that she was so close to that date, she didn't hear anything.

There were many wealthy people out there, that sold stockpile Armageddon gear, that were keeping a low profile these days. They may have to deal with going out of business. She just knew that out there somewhere, had to exist the technology that right now, is only in our imaginations. If this is so, then, who is pulling all the strings that are keeping all of these new technologies a secret? What would motivate someone to keep all of these things at bay, if they knew that they were the answer to some of the world's problems. For some reason, these space crafts are drawn to nuclear missiles. They must think that humans are a very stupid race. There really is no point in anything, when considering nuclear weapons. Shirley had grown very familiar with the nuclear missile threat.

It was eery to live under that kind of pressure. The media

reflected that very dilemma every day. These were the messages of total world annihilation that she knew in her teen years. It was a very real threat at the time. Now with so many decades that have passed, people don't really think about the concept behind the motivation of nuclear war. Somehow society had positioned that grave possibility, into the background. Well the evidence suggests that, the aliens are more than well aware of the motivations, behind nuclear bombs. There was a recognition within, of the possibility that there are solutions, to our problems. Can we all just collectively disappear, just like the Incas did? The prophets contend, that is a definite possible outcome, if we don't find a way to try to maintain a peaceful co-existence.

The masks needed to come off, if humanity could withstand the amount of blows that have occurred. through injustice. Darwin really had something when he described his whole, survival of the fittest theory. There is a certain regimen that comes with living. That the power comes from believing in the unknown, is what Shirley had come to know. This did not have to take on a cult like personification, in real life. People can absorb things into their lives, without having to go all crazy about it. The more that people took on the role of the one who persists in their convincing; are those that are the least convincing.

These people are easy to spot. They act like exaggerated cartoon characters. Some of them even look like cartoon characters.

Another thing that drives people to succeed is the comfort that it can bring, as well as the flexibility. Shirley had to claim her comfortable passage through this world. Greed doesn't meet any standards. The losers are the people, who rubbed their success up under other people's noses. This may be taken quiet literally. We all invite excess, especially early on in life. These bouts of excess fade in their effectiveness. People could stage what their lives are to be. She was certain though, for herself, that she was not ready earlier. Some people have the advantage of dealing with things quicker than others. Ours is not to ask why. The sooner we own the failure, it seemed the faster that we can achieve success. Failure need not be a humiliating experience.

Nothing could slow down the healing process quicker than the fear of failure. We catapult ourselves into the intangible realms by trying to have control over the metaphysical. Things just need to be sometimes. Life is about those enduring moments that are frozen in time. They are there to remind us of who we are. We can enable the future generations, with our knowledge. Not afraid of being trite, either. Never be your own worst enemy. Take into account common courtesy. Never borrow what you can not give back. Realize that you have time on your side.

Take an inventory of what you want to achieve. Be joyful as much as you can. Put a smile on that face; it is the first thing that other people will notice. Everyone in the human race looks angry now, that we can't smile in our passport photos. Its clear that everyone looks a lot better when they smile. Make laughter as natural as brushing your teeth. Do not under any circumstances, take yourself seriously. She had seen this happen to people. They were uncomfortable.

Don't be sanctimonious, it is so annoying. People who rise up on to the pulpit, going around telling everyone within 20 miles, what they should do. Shirley thought that what they did was vulgar. It was so obvious, that they had to run others down to a level, that they were able to relate to. Don't just follow everything in society like a sheep. It is admirable to take steps towards doing something about what goes on.

As Canadians, we have the power to see behind the mire. It is better to give than to receive. That was one of those old adages that nailed it! Never run out of ideas. Don't back away from a challenge, but don't show violence when things don't work out the way that they should.

Logic does not come into play all the time necessarily. Be open to strange new things. Throughout her life, she had come to enjoy doing things that she never thought that she should enjoy. There always exists the element of surprise. Elation is as natural as air, is to breathe. She hadn't gone down that typical tried, and true path.

What is more typical to her now, are the twists, and turns, down that life path. Experiences sometimes started off being simple. All of humanity have the propensities toward some sort of, destructive nature. Shirley had seen it time, and again in people in her life.

She owned it, and accounted for it. The only person you can not fool, is yourself.

Every one of us should brush up, and upgrade our skills. The technological advances spanning from the time of Shirley's birth in 1967, to the present year of 2012, have come at a much faster pace than was anticipated. Knowledge was spilling out through loads of outlets. Information had become big business. The masses had to educate themselves about what to do with all that knowledge. If man could pour as much money as possible into knowledge, this world could prosper. Never mind this sinister marketplace that sells human organs. We have found that technology can fix a lot of things, that are wrong. It does not have to be a treacherous climb up to the ladder of knowledge. Shirley refused to see it that way.

People can adopt to ways of making knowledge more accessible, but can they actually use that knowledge, in a constructive way? There were a lot of sleazy people in business. What is there left to exploit? Sage advice can help enlighten the masses. But what is this all about? The vibrations off the coast of Vancouver Island, have been on her mind as of late. This was the area right now, where the ocean is showing significant changes. A government of Canada commercial runs, that shows the tug boats, and watch guard coast workers, making sure that oil, doesn't spill. Haven't those people tired of all that drilling? Life was a delicate balancing act. Were we the stars of our own circus? That's what life seemed to be for Shirley, was just one big circus. It was no wonder that she felt a pull when she saw the 'Jazz Series' by Matisse.

We, all of us, must have a narrative. It is just fine, not to agree.

She had enjoyed escaping into the Shakespearean landscapes of Star Trek, where there was also an abundance of drama.

Fabricated drama had become somewhat of a hobby. Indulgences should not become customary. This would rule out any sort of compelling reason to live. The jilt that happens when we first wake up, worked best for Shirley. This was her at her most productive. It made her wonder just how much people missed out on, when they slept all day. Theirs is a dimly lit world in which they interact at a different speed. The time to rest, shouldn't have to be measured. She agreed that people needed as much rest as they got. She had taken all the rest she needed. She had experienced that lucid zombie, zone, of sleep deprivation, where nothing made sense.

In order to love, you need no prerequisites. Shirley had allowed the feeling of love to go through every level of her being. It was a wonderful experience. The worst part about the high feeling of roller coaster love, is the come down. It's like coming down hard, off of drugs. She was thankful for having stayed away from what she viewed as the dirty drugs. Other people, not her, did that sort of thing. She could never buy into that. So from that she had concluded that it never hurt to nurture your mind. So what if she was a mature adult now? To be an observant explorer was the meaning of life, as we know it here, in this dimension.

As humans we can not function as computers. Computers were depicted as monsters in the 1980s. Shirley bought into that early on, but gradually things changed. The world needs a humanistic view at all times. This will ensure that we do not stray from our values. Too much interaction with computers, has caused this rift between people. This could not have been predicted. She had observed that computers had become an essential part of people's lives. Suspicious thoughts have to be put aside to get over people living in social isolation. There were times, when solitude can help to cleanse the soul. Whatever was happening; computers had somehow been the portal to it. The establishment of a plan, should be decided upon early on. She felt that she could have made more use of her time, if she had figured out the formula. It wasn't to the level of discontent. The dirty dogs had their time.

It was with pride that Shirley could now look back on time, and be at peace with her results. She wanted to fully participate in finding solutions. One way of getting things done, isn't necessarily the same as another person's way, of getting things done. There's always a fun way to do things. She knew she had not yet exhausted all of her repertoire. Rome was not built in one day. Shirley had roamed the streets of Rome, and the message was quiet clear. The destruction infused in greed, had been responsible for the fall of the Roman Empire. The speculations persist. Be compelled to be persistent in all that you can achieve. There were spectacular views that she had chosen to see. Shirley, is myself.

Made in the USA
Charleston, SC
09 September 2014